PHILIPPE THIRAULT 上海梦 JORGE MIGUEL

SHANGHAI DREAM

Life Drawn

PHILIPPE THIRAULT
Writer

Based on a screenplay by
EDWARD RYAN and **YANG XIE**

JORGE MIGUEL
Artist

DELF
Colorist

⸎

MARK BENCE
Translator

⸎

FABRICE SAPOLSKY and **ALEX DONOGHUE**
US Edition Editors

AMANDA LUCIDO
Assistant Editor

CAMILLE THÉLOT-VERNOUX and **BRUNO LECIGNE**
Original Edition Editors

JERRY FRISSEN
Senior Art Director

FABRICE GIGER
Publisher

With special thanks to Pierre Spengler.

Rights and Licensing - licensing@humanoids.com
Press and Social Media - pr@humanoids.com

UFA STUDIOS, BERLIN, NOVEMBER 9, 1938...

LOOK AT THIS SYMBOL CARVED INTO THE WALL OF THE 1000-YEAR-OLD TEMPLE!

THIS PROVES THAT THE REICH WILL ALSO LIVE FOR 1000 YEARS!

CUT! THAT'S A WRAP!

BERNHARD? WHY ARE YOU HERE?

YOU'RE INSANE TO HAVE COME. HOW DID YOU EVEN GET IN?

I WORKED FOR THE STUDIOS FOR EIGHT YEARS, MANFRED. I KNEW EVERY NOOK AND CRANNY...UNTIL I GOT *KICKED OUT*, THAT IS.

I'M NOT THE ONE WHO INVENTED RACIAL LAWS. YOU WERE A VERY GOOD ASSISTANT DIRECTOR. I EVEN WANTED TO LET YOU TRY YOUR HAND AT DIRECTING.

LOOK... I DIDN'T COME HERE TO BLAME ANYONE, JUST TO OFFER YOU A SCRIPT THAT ILLO HAS WRITTEN. IT'S A ROMANTIC COMEDY SET IN BERLIN.

ER-- AND HOW IS ILLO?

LIKE A SCREENWRITER WHO'S BEEN BANNED FROM WORKING FOR FOUR YEARS... SHE'S BRAVE, BUT LIFE IS TOUGH FOR US. WE'VE HAD TO MOVE IN WITH HER FATHER.

IF YOU WERE TO BUY HER SCRIPT, YOU'D NOT ONLY BE DOING US A FAVOR, BUT ILLO WOULD FEEL AS IF HER LIFE MEANT SOMETHING AGAIN.

WILDE NACHT IN BERLIN*...

YOU KNOW IT WOULD BE *ILLEGAL* FOR ME TO EMPLOY A JEW.

OFFICIALLY, THE SCRIPT WOULDN'T BE BY ILLO, OF COURSE. WE'D ARRANGE IT SECRETLY.

ILLO IS VERY TALENTED. I HAVE NO DOUBT IT'S EXCELLENT, BUT IT'S TOO DANGEROUS. PEOPLE MIGHT FIND OUT.

TAKE YOUR SCRIPT BACK, BERNHARD. I'M TERRIBLY SORRY.

NO! PLEASE, JUST GIVE ME A FEW MORE MINUTES OF YOUR TIME.

ALL YOU MAKE ARE PROPAGANDA MOVIES, BUT PEOPLE NEED TO BE *ENTERTAINED*, TOO! IT'S A REALLY GOOD STORY; A HYMN TO LOVE; LIGHT-HEARTED AND FULL OF IDEAS. LET ME GIVE YOU A BRIEF SYNOPSIS...

*WILD NIGHT IN BERLIN

4

"IT'S THE STORY OF IDA, A YOUNG WOMAN BORED WITH LIFE IN HER SMALL PROVINCIAL TOWN. ONE DAY, SHE HAS TO GO TO BERLIN FOR THE FUNERAL OF AN AUNT, WHOSE LAST WILL AND TESTAMENT HAS NAMED HER AS A BENEFICIARY..."

TO MY NIECE, IDA NEUMANN, I LEAVE MY RESIDENCE IN BERLIN, TOGETHER WITH ALL OF ITS CONTENTS: FURNITURE, OBJECTS AND WORKS OF ART. THE EIGHT SERVANTS WILL ALSO REMAIN, IF SHE SO DESIRES.

"ON HER WAY BACK TO THE STATION, IDA GLANCES INTO A SHOP WINDOW AND HER EYE FALLS ON A STUNNING DRESS..."

"KURT, A YOUNG MAN FROM AN ENTIRELY DIFFERENT BACKGROUND, HAPPENS TO BE PASSING BY, BUT IT'S IDA THAT HE FINDS STUNNING..."

"AFTER SHE'S VISITED THE SHOP, THEN LISTENED TO ALL OF KURT'S BANTER, IDA MISSES HER TRAIN HOME..."

"SO IDA LETS KURT WHISK HER OFF INTO THE WHIRLWIND OF BERLIN LIFE ON A SERIES OF WILD ESCAPADES INTENDED TO WIN HER HEART..."

3

IT'S JUST NOT POSSIBLE, BERNHARD. I HAVEN'T BEEN IN CHARGE OF THESE STUDIOS FOR A LONG WHILE NOW...

HE HAS.

MANFRED, LISTEN! I BEG YOU!

AND I'M BEGGING YOU TO LEAVE MY OFFICE. LEAVE THE STUDIOS WITHOUT BEING SPOTTED. I'M COUNTING ON YOU, AND I ASK THAT YOU NOT RETURN. YOU PUT ME AT RISK.

MANFRED, THE MINISTRY OF PROPAGANDA JUST RANG. THEY'RE VERY PLEASED WITH UFA'S LATEST FILMS. THEY'RE PLEASED WITH US, AND PLEASED WITH YOU!

I'M VERY GLAD...

4

ORANIENBURGER STRASSE, BERLIN'S MAIN JEWISH QUARTER...

MY REGARDS, HERR KESSLER, AND HAVE A PLEASANT EVENING.

THANK YOU, EZER. GOODNIGHT.

STOP THAT, ILLO. YOU'RE GOING TO RUIN YOUR EYES!

AND WHERE'S YOUR HUSBAND? HE'S ALWAYS LATE.

HE'LL BE BACK. WITH GOOD NEWS, HOPEFULLY.

WHY DOES THE ALMIGHTY ALLOW THAT MY DAUGHTER BE FORCED INTO JOBS THAT ARE BENEATH HER DIGNITY?

BUT THIS WORK ALLOWS ME TO MAINTAIN MY DIGNITY, PAPA.

CLOSING TIME, GENTLEMEN. DRINK UP NOW, AND BE CAREFUL ON THE WAY HOME...

ILLO... HOW DISAPPOINTED SHE'LL BE...

NAZI BASTARDS. YOU'RE ONLY THRIVING BECAUSE OF HATE AND COWARDICE.

MOM, I'M AFRAID!

JUST RUN AND DON'T LOOK BACK!

THEY'RE LIKE WILD ANIMALS!

WHAT HAPPENED? LET ME HELP YOU--

GET OFF ME!

YOU OUGHTTA RUN, TOO! THEY'RE KILLING JEWS!

THEY'RE OUT TO DESTROY EVERYTHING!

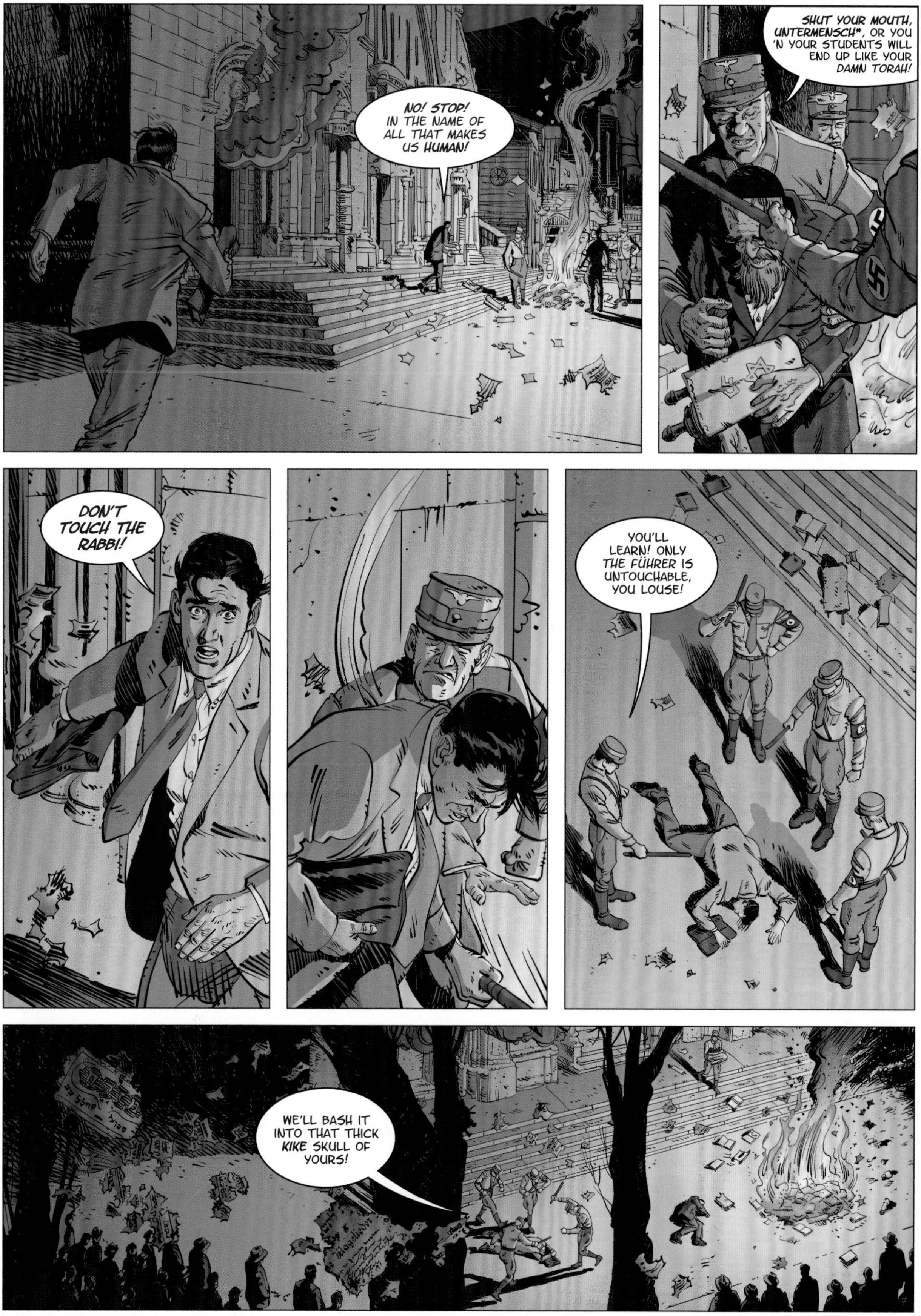
NO! STOP! IN THE NAME OF ALL THAT MAKES US HUMAN!
SHUT YOUR MOUTH, UNTERMENSCH*, OR YOU 'N YOUR STUDENTS WILL END UP LIKE YOUR DAMN TORAH!
DON'T TOUCH THE RABBI!
YOU'LL LEARN! ONLY THE FÜHRER IS UNTOUCHABLE, YOU LOUSE!
WE'LL BASH IT INTO THAT THICK KIKE SKULL OF YOURS!

*A PERSON CONSIDERED RACIALLY OR SOCIALLY INFERIOR.

WHAT'VE YOU GOT HIDDEN IN HERE? YOU SEEM ATTACHED TO IT...

IF IT'S WORTH ANYTHING, IT GOES IN OUR POCKETS. IF NOT—INTO THE FIRE!

NO-O-O! ILLO'S SCREENPLAY!

BASTARDS!

YOU SCUMBAGS!

AFTER HIM!

10

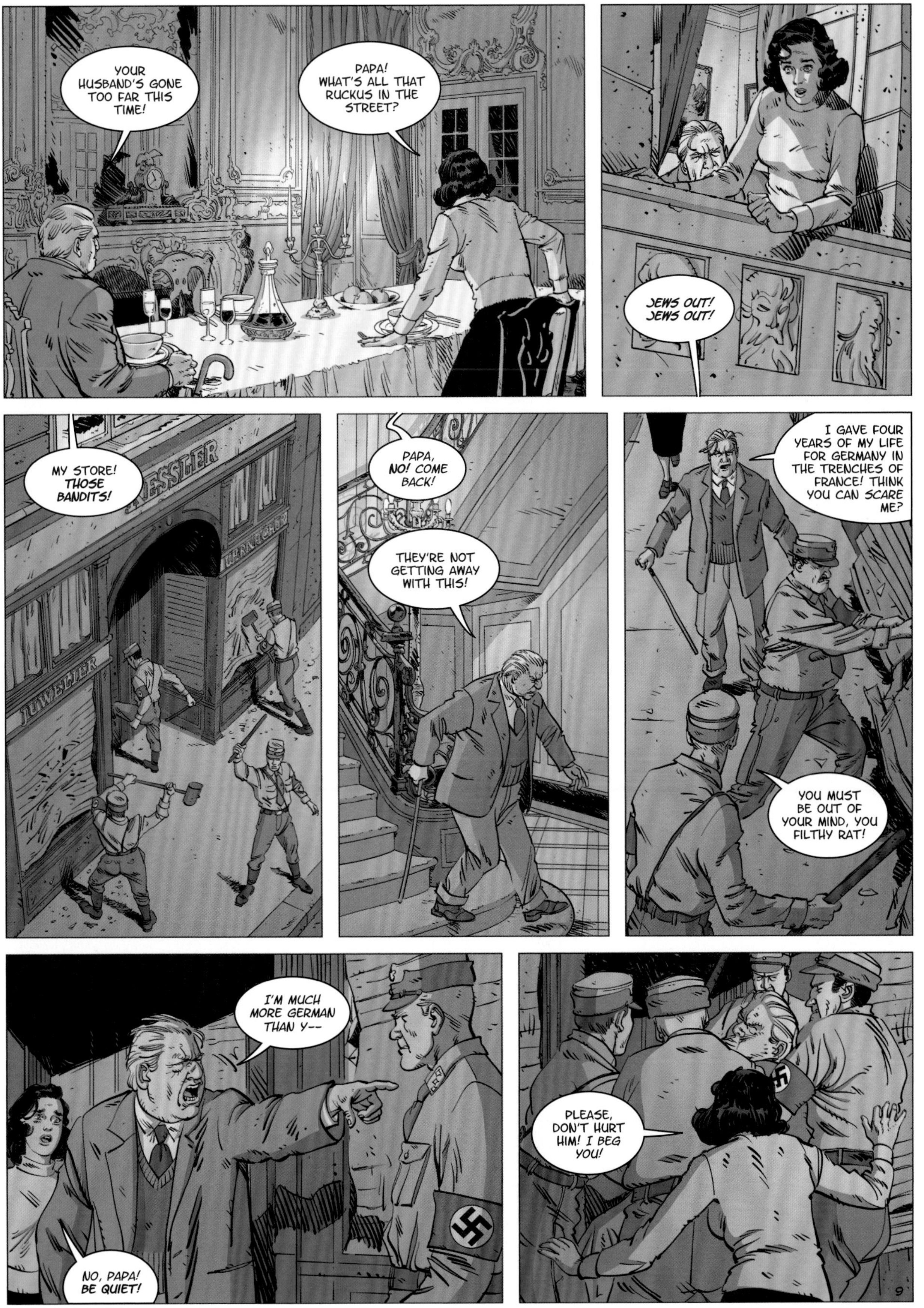
YOUR HUSBAND'S GONE TOO FAR THIS TIME!
PAPA! WHAT'S ALL THAT RUCKUS IN THE STREET?
JEWS OUT! JEWS OUT!
MY STORE! THOSE BANDITS!
KESSLER
JUWELIER
PAPA, NO! COME BACK!
THEY'RE NOT GETTING AWAY WITH THIS!
I GAVE FOUR YEARS OF MY LIFE FOR GERMANY IN THE TRENCHES OF FRANCE! THINK YOU CAN SCARE ME?
YOU MUST BE OUT OF YOUR MIND, YOU FILTHY RAT!
I'M MUCH MORE GERMAN THAN Y--
NO, PAPA! BE QUIET!
PLEASE, DON'T HURT HIM! I BEG YOU!

ENOUGH! LEAVE THEM.

GO TO AUGUSTSTRASSE. THAT'S AN ORDER!

FICHT?!

AS IF JOINING THOSE BASTARDS WASN'T ENOUGH FOR YOU, NOW YOU'RE DOING THEIR DIRTY WORK...

HOLD YOUR TONGUE, KESSLER, OR IT MIGHT GET CUT OFF — JUST LIKE YOUR LEG.

I LOST MY LEG SAVING YOU AT VERDUN, FICHT! DON'T TELL ME YOU'VE FORGOTTEN.

LET'S GO HOME, PAPA. THEY MIGHT COME BACK.

I DIDN'T FORGET A THING, AND THAT'S WHY YOU'RE GETTING AWAY WITH THIS TONIGHT. BUT DON'T PUSH YOUR LUCK. I WARNED YOU BEFORE TO SELL YOUR BUSINESS WHILE YOU STILL COULD.

IT'S ALL OVER HERE FOR YOU JEWS. THERE'S NO ROOM FOR YOU MONEY-GRUBBERS IN THE REICH.

BERNHARD!

I... I MANAGED TO GET AWAY...

A WORD OF ADVICE: WHATEVER HAPPENS, DON'T GO OUT FOR THE NEXT TWO DAYS...

12

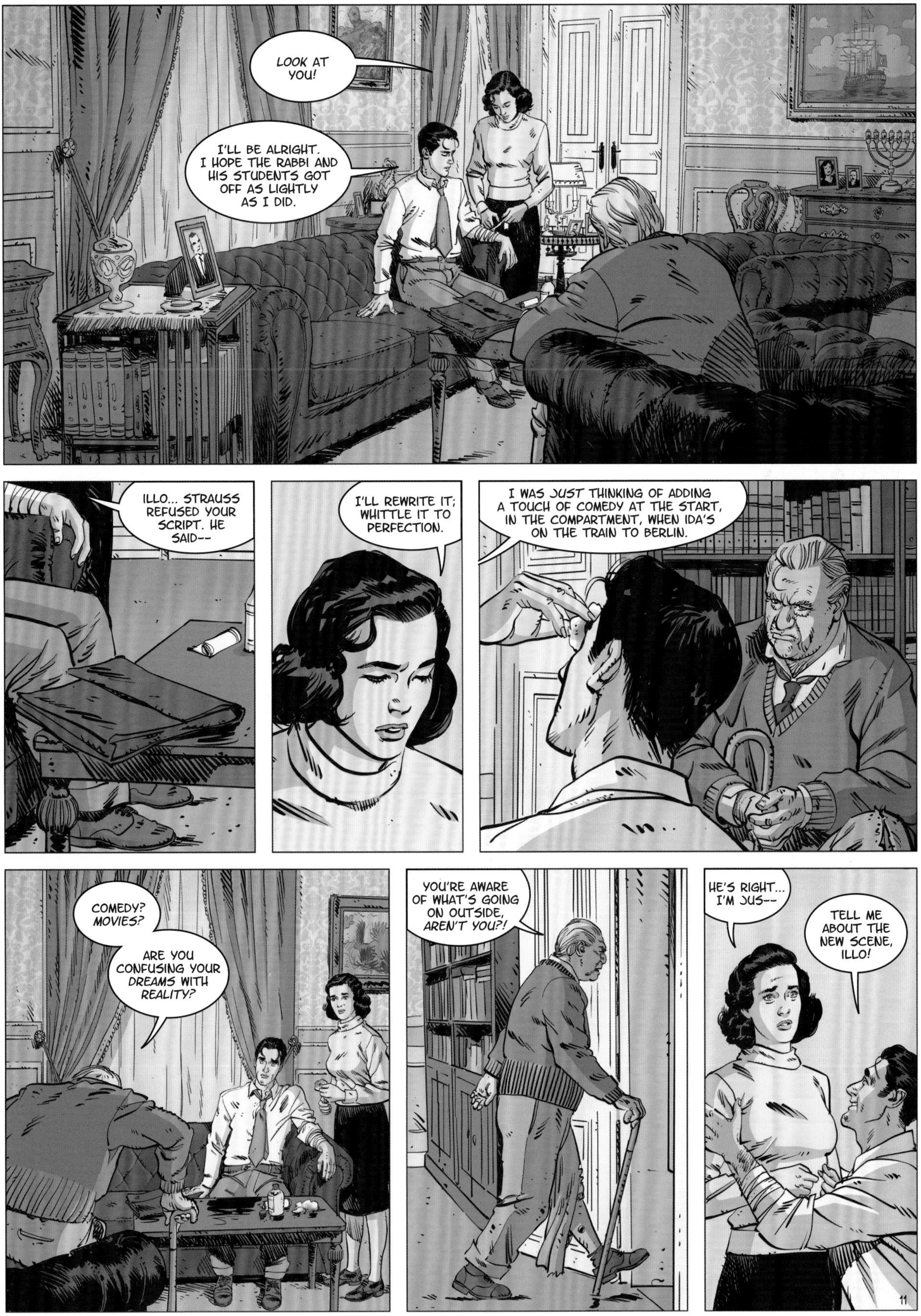
LOOK AT YOU!
I'LL BE ALRIGHT. I HOPE THE RABBI AND HIS STUDENTS GOT OFF AS LIGHTLY AS I DID.
ILLO... STRAUSS REFUSED YOUR SCRIPT. HE SAID--
I'LL REWRITE IT; WHITTLE IT TO PERFECTION.
I WAS JUST THINKING OF ADDING A TOUCH OF COMEDY AT THE START, IN THE COMPARTMENT, WHEN IDA'S ON THE TRAIN TO BERLIN.
COMEDY? MOVIES?
ARE YOU CONFUSING YOUR DREAMS WITH REALITY?
YOU'RE AWARE OF WHAT'S GOING ON OUTSIDE, AREN'T YOU?!
HE'S RIGHT... I'M JUS--
TELL ME ABOUT THE NEW SCENE, ILLO!
11

GET THIS FOUL THING OFF OF ME!

I'M TERRIBLY EMBARRASSED...

CLUMSY FOOL! THIS IS UNBELIEVABLE!

THAT'S MUCH BETTER.

BUT IT WON'T KEEP MY SCRIPT FROM LANDING IN A DRAWER.

I PROMISE, YOUR SCREENPLAY WILL GET MADE ONE DAY, AND I'M GOING TO DIRECT IT!

THUD!

12

PAPA!

NO-- HE STAYS *OUTSIDE!* AND SHUT THAT DOOR.

I WON'T LET HIM SEE ME HELPLESS LIKE THIS.

BESIDES, I DON'T NEED ANY HELP!

THIS LEG IS *USELESS!* JUST SOMETHING ELSE THAT NEEDS REPLACING...

... I FEEL GUILTY, YOU KNOW. I WAS THE ONE WHO REFUSED TO LEAVE BERLIN. IT'S MY FAULT THAT WE DIDN'T EMIGRATE TO AMERICA WHEN WE STILL COULD.

I'M SURE YOU AND YOUR HUSBAND COULD HAVE HAD A CAREER IN THE MOVIES OVER THERE.

IT'S NOT TOO LATE, PAPA.

BUT TONIGHT SHOULD SERVE AS OUR LAST WARNING. WE NEED TO LEAVE.

IF ONLY THINGS WERE THAT SIMPLE... A LOT OF PEOPLE COUNT ON ME HERE. WHAT WILL HAPPEN TO MY EMPLOYEES? TAKE EZER: HE'S ALWAYS WORKED FOR ME. WE ARE HIS ONLY FAMILY. I CAN'T JUST GO OFF AND ABANDON HIM LIKE THAT.

THEN LET'S TAKE EZER WITH US.

13

TWO DAYS LATER...

Jacob Rosenberg

ILLO, WHY ARE THESE PEOPLE HERE?

THE NAZIS HAVE BROKEN INTO THE APARTMENTS OF EVERY JEWISH FAMILY ON OUR STREET, EXCEPT OURS. THEY HAVE LISTS OF NAMES! AND THOUSANDS OF JEWISH MEN HAVE BEEN ARRESTED... THESE PEOPLE WOULD LIKE TO STAY WITH US... THEY'RE AFRAID AND THEY THINK THEY'D BE SAFER HERE.

HERR KESSLER, YOU'RE A HERO OF THE GREAT WAR! FIRST CLASS, WITH AN IRON CROSS. THOSE BANDITS WOULDN'T DARE TO ATTACK YOU OR YOUR FAMILY--

AND MY WORKERS? AREN'T THEY MY FAMILY, TOO? BUT KUPPERSTOCK AND SCHOENFELD STILL GOT ARRESTED!

I'M GOING DOWN TO THE JDC. THEY'LL HELP US. IT'S THEIR JOB, AFTER ALL.

WAIT. I'LL COME WITH YOU.

NO! I'LL GO ALONE! AFTER YOUR EXPLOITS AT THE SYNAGOGUE, YOU MIGHT BE SPOTTED.

*THE AMERICAN JEWISH JOINT DISTRIBUTION COMMITTEE, ALSO REFERRED TO AS "THE JOINT" AND "THE JDC," IS A JEWISH RELIEF ORGANIZATION, FOUNDED IN 1914, DURING WORLD WAR I.

FRAU HERSCH, TWO YEARS AGO YOU RECEIVED THREE MIGRANT VISAS FOR THE UNITED STATES AND THE DOCUMENTS NEEDED TO LEAVE THE REICH, BUT YOU ALLOWED THEM ALL TO EXPIRE.

GIVEN THE RECENT EVENTS, TENS OF THOUSANDS OF PEOPLE NOW WISH TO LEAVE. YOU MUST UNDERSTAND, YOU'RE NO LONGER A PRIORITY. SO, IF YOU'LL EXCUSE ME--

I SWEAR IT WASN'T SOME WHIM OR OVERSIGHT OF MINE, HERR EHRENTHAL. AT THE LAST MINUTE, MY FATHER REFUSED TO LEAVE GERMANY. HE SIMPLY WOULDN'T LISTEN. HE'S *DISABLED*, SIR.

I COULDN'T JUST LEAVE HIM ON HIS OWN.

I SUGGESTED THAT MY HUSBAND GO ALONE, BUT HE DIDN'T WANT TO LEAVE ME, EVEN WHEN I PROMISED TO COME AND JOIN HIM LATER.

EVERY FAMILY HAS ITS SHARE OF BAD LUCK, FRAU HERSCH. I'M SORRY YOU COULDN'T CONVINCE YOUR FATHER.

BE HUMAN... DON'T SEND ME AWAY WITHOUT A GLIMMER OF HOPE...EVEN THE FAINTEST. HELP ME... PLEASE.

LISTEN... YOU'D NEED TO START OVER FROM SCRATCH: FIND SOME GUARANTORS IN AMERICA OR GET A FEW JOB OFFERS IN ENGLAND. ONLY *THEN* COULD YOU ACQUIRE PERMITS TO LEAVE THE REICH.

YES, WE CAN GET LETTERS OF SUPPORT! WE KNOW PEOPLE IN THE MOVIE BUSINESS OVER THERE, IN HOLLYWOOD! FRIENDS WHO EMIGRATED!

DON'T GET CARRIED AWAY. THE PROCESS TAKES TIME.

HOW LONG?

A YEAR, MAYBE MORE.

17

OK... SIT DOWN AND LISTEN, BUT THIS REMAINS *STRICTLY* BETWEEN THE TWO OF US.

THE ASSASSINATION OF THE DIPLOMAT VOM RATH WAS ONLY A *PRETEXT* FOR THESE LATEST RAIDS. NEXT TIME, THE NAZIS WON'T EVEN BOTHER LOOKING FOR EXCUSES. THIS COUNTRY WILL SOON BECOME A LIVING HELL FOR THE JEWS.

IF I WERE YOU, I'D TRY TO ESCAPE IN SECRET TO FRANCE OR HOLLAND.

AND FROM THERE WE COULD TRAVEL ONWARDS TO AMERICA... IF YOU'RE MENTIONING IT, THEN YOU *MUST KNOW* OF SOME SECRET WAY TO LEAVE THE COUNTRY, DON'T YOU?

YES. I COULD GIVE YOU A CONTACT, BUT IT WOULD BE DANGEROUS. YOU'D HAVE TO BE PREPARED TO WALK FOR SEVERAL HOURS TO CROSS THE BORDER AT NIGHT...

HERR EHRENTHAL, I TOLD YOU THAT MY FATHER IS HANDICAPPED! HE WOULDN'T LAST HALF AN HOUR.

IN THAT CASE, IF YOU HAVE THE MEANS, THERE IS ONE LAST HOPE: GO SOMEWHERE THAT DOESN'T REQUIRE A VISA. THERE IS SUCH A COUNTRY.

BUT IT'S NOT EXACTLY *THE LAND OF PLENTY.* QUITE THE CONTRARY: IT'S A MISERABLE LIFE, A TOUGH CLIMATE, AND SICKNESS IS RIFE.

HERE? ARE YOU SURE?

SHANGHAI?

IT'S THE HOLLYWOOD OF THE FAR EAST! I CAN WORK OVER THERE UNTIL WE ALL EMIGRATE TO THE U.S.

BUT THE REGION IS AT WAR.

THE CITY'S UNDER JAPANESE CONTROL, BUT WE'D LIVE IN THE INTERNATIONAL SETTLEMENT. AND, AS BERNHARD SAID, IT'D ONLY BE TEMPORARY.

NEVERTHELESS, WE STILL NEED TO FIND A WAY TO GET TICKETS ON A LINER THAT SAILS THERE.

I'LL DEAL WITH THAT.

I'LL CONTACT FRAU AUER. SINCE THE RACIAL LAWS WERE PASSED, SHE DOESN'T EVEN DARE TO SAY "HELLO" IN THE STREET ANYMORE. BUT I HELPED HER AND HER HUSBAND BUY THEIR TRAVEL AGENCY. SHE CAN'T REFUSE MY REQUEST.

CHINESE... JAPANESE... THAT'S FINE BY ME! REMEMBER HOW WE LOVED THAT FILM ABOUT THE TWO KIDS WHO REALIZED THEIR FATHER WASN'T ANYBODY IMPORTANT?

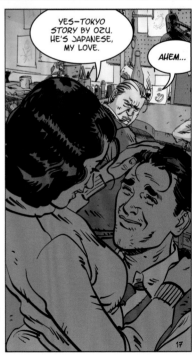

YES—TOKYO STORY BY OZU. HE'S JAPANESE, MY LOVE.

AHEM...

17

GOOD DAY, LADIES.

FRAU AUER, WHY HAVEN'T YOU REPLIED TO ANY OF MY MESSAGES OVER THE PAST THREE WEEKS?

COME INTO MY OFFICE, HERR KESSLER.

YOU WERE A FRIEND OF MY WIFE'S. TODAY SHE IS NO LONGER WITH US, BUT TWENTY YEARS AGO I HELPED YOU. I'M SIMPLY ASKING YOU TO RETURN THE FAVOR. I PROMISE IT'LL BE THE FIRST AND LAST THING I EVER ASK OF YOU.

WELL, I'M TRULY SORRY... BUT ALL THE BOAT TICKETS TO FAR EAST DESTINATIONS WERE SOLD OUT TEN MONTHS IN ADVANCE. AND THERE ARE ALREADY LONG WAITING LISTS FOR ANY SPOTS THAT MAY BECOME AVAILABLE.

DID YOU HEAR WHAT I SAID, HERR KESSLER?

...WAS THERE SOMETHING ELSE?

I'VE WAITED TWENTY YEARS TO ASK YOU A FAVOR...

I'LL STAY HERE UNTIL I DIE, IF NEED BE.

...

I'LL SEE WHAT I CAN DO... I'LL BE IN TOUCH.

EVENING, EZER.

EVENING, FRÄULEIN ILLO. EVENING, HERR BERNHARD.

THIS JEWELRY BELONGED TO OUR MOTHERS. WE DECIDED NOT TO LIST IT IN THE INVENTORY THE NAZIS FORCED US TO WRITE, AND WE DID THE RIGHT THING.

BUT... FRAU KESSLER'S JEWELRY?! NO, YOU CAN'T DO THAT... WHAT FOR? WE DON'T EVEN KNOW IF WE'LL BE ABLE TO LEAVE YET!

YES, WE ARE LEAVING! EVERY LITTLE BIT COUNTS NOW. WE'RE ONLY ALLOWED TO LEAVE GERMANY WITH TEN MARKS IN OUR POCKETS, A WATCH AND A RING, SO WE HAVE TO BE CRAFTY.

HERE'S ALL THE GOLD LEFT OVER FOR REPAIRS. THIS POT CONTAINS GOLD DUST FROM OUR LAST MONTHS OF WORK. IT'S UP TO YOU NOW, EZER.

HOW LONG DO YOU THINK IT WILL TAKE TO MAKE WHAT WE ASK OF YOU?

SEVERAL DAYS, HERR BERNHARD.

19

21

ILLO, DARLING, COME AND SEE!

WHAT ARE YOU DOING?

LOOK! LOOK CLOSELY... THE EYELETS ARE SOLID GOLD, ALL EIGHT OF THEM! EZER COATED THEM WITH BLACK PAINT AND—PRESTO! A BIT MORE GOLD LEAVES GERMANY, RIGHT UNDER THE NAZIS' NOSES!

HERE'S YOUR BELT. THE BUCKLE'S MADE OF PAINTED GOLD, TOO.

HASN'T EZER DONE A FINE JOB?

YES, BUT THE BUCKLE IS EVER SO HEAVY! I'LL PACK IT IN MY SUITCASE.

THAT GOLD WILL LET US TRAVEL ON TO THE U.S. FROM CHINA.

WE'LL HAVE TO ADAPT THE SCRIPT AND SET IT IN NEW YORK. FIND A TYPICALLY AMERICAN NAME FOR IDA AND A CLASSIC AMERICAN HICK TOWN INSTEAD OF HER GERMAN VILLAGE...

I'VE ALREADY THOUGHT OF THAT! I'LL CALL HER EMMA...

AND HE'LL BE FRANK, AS IN CAPRA.

NO, THE GENOA-SHANGHAI LINERS ARE FULLY BOOKED FOR THE NEXT TEN MONTHS.

HOWEVER, THERE IS A WAY TO GET TO THE TOP OF THE COMPANY'S WAITING LISTS...

THE WIFE OF THE DIRECTOR OF THE GERMAN SHIPPING COMPANY THAT PLIES THE SHANGHAI ROUTE IS A FRIEND. A WELL-EDUCATED LADY OF EXQUISITE ARTISTIC TASTE...

I'M SURE THESE THREE LITTLE IMPRESSIONIST PAINTINGS WOULD PLEASE HER IMMENSELY.

I... I AGREE.

YOU WOULD, OF COURSE, HAVE TO PAY FOR THE TICKETS— ROUND TRIP.

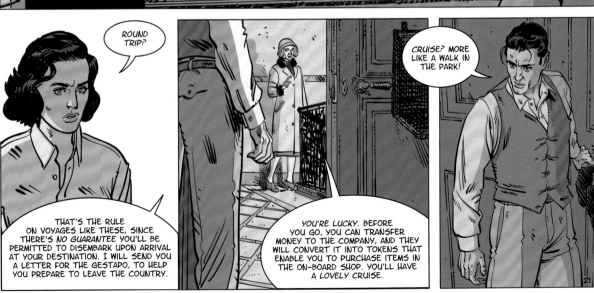

ROUND TRIP?

THAT'S THE RULE ON VOYAGES LIKE THESE, SINCE THERE'S NO GUARANTEE YOU'LL BE PERMITTED TO DISEMBARK UPON ARRIVAL AT YOUR DESTINATION. I WILL SEND YOU A LETTER FOR THE GESTAPO, TO HELP YOU PREPARE TO LEAVE THE COUNTRY.

YOU'RE LUCKY. BEFORE YOU GO, YOU CAN TRANSFER MONEY TO THE COMPANY, AND THEY WILL CONVERT IT INTO TOKENS THAT ENABLE YOU TO PURCHASE ITEMS IN THE ON-BOARD SHOP. YOU'LL HAVE A LOVELY CRUISE.

CRUISE? MORE LIKE A WALK IN THE PARK!

21

THREE WEEKS LATER...

ARE YOU SURE? THERE *MUST* BE A WAY! NO? LISTEN, I... VERY WELL. ALRIGHT... THANKS...

CHILDREN, I'VE JUST BEEN TOLD THAT THERE'S A FREE CABIN ON THE SHIP SAILING OUT OF GENOA IN A WEEK. SADLY, THERE ARE ONLY TWO BERTHS LEFT.

YOU TWO WILL TAKE THEM.

THAT'S OUT OF THE QUESTION, PAPA! I *WON'T* LEAVE YOU BEHIND!

YES, ILLO, YOU AND YOUR FATHER CAN GO FIRST. EZER AND I WILL JOIN YOU AS SOON AS WE CAN.

DON'T YOU SEE? THERE WON'T BE ANY MORE TICKETS OR FAVORS WITHOUT PAYING AGAIN, AND WE'VE NOTHING LEFT TO BARGAIN WITH.

THERE'S THE GOLD! THE BELT, THE EYELETS--

THAT GOLD'S UNDECLARED. IF THE AUTHORITIES FOUND OUT, THEY'D ARREST US.

IT'LL BE OKAY. ALL CHILDREN MUST LEAVE THEIR PARENTS SOMEDAY.

COME ON NOW, NO TIME TO LOSE. PACK YOUR SUITCASES QUICKLY AND CAREFULLY. YOU'LL NEED TO PASS THE CUSTOMS INSPECTION.

22

ONE LEATHER BELT WITH A METAL BUCKLE.

PASSE UND PAP...

ONE PAIR OF MEN'S LEATHER SHOES, SIZE 10.

THAT'S A SCREENPLAY-- IT'S LISTED IN THE INVENTORY.

IS IT SOME JEWISH STORY?

ALRIGHT, YOU CAN SEAL IT UP.

23

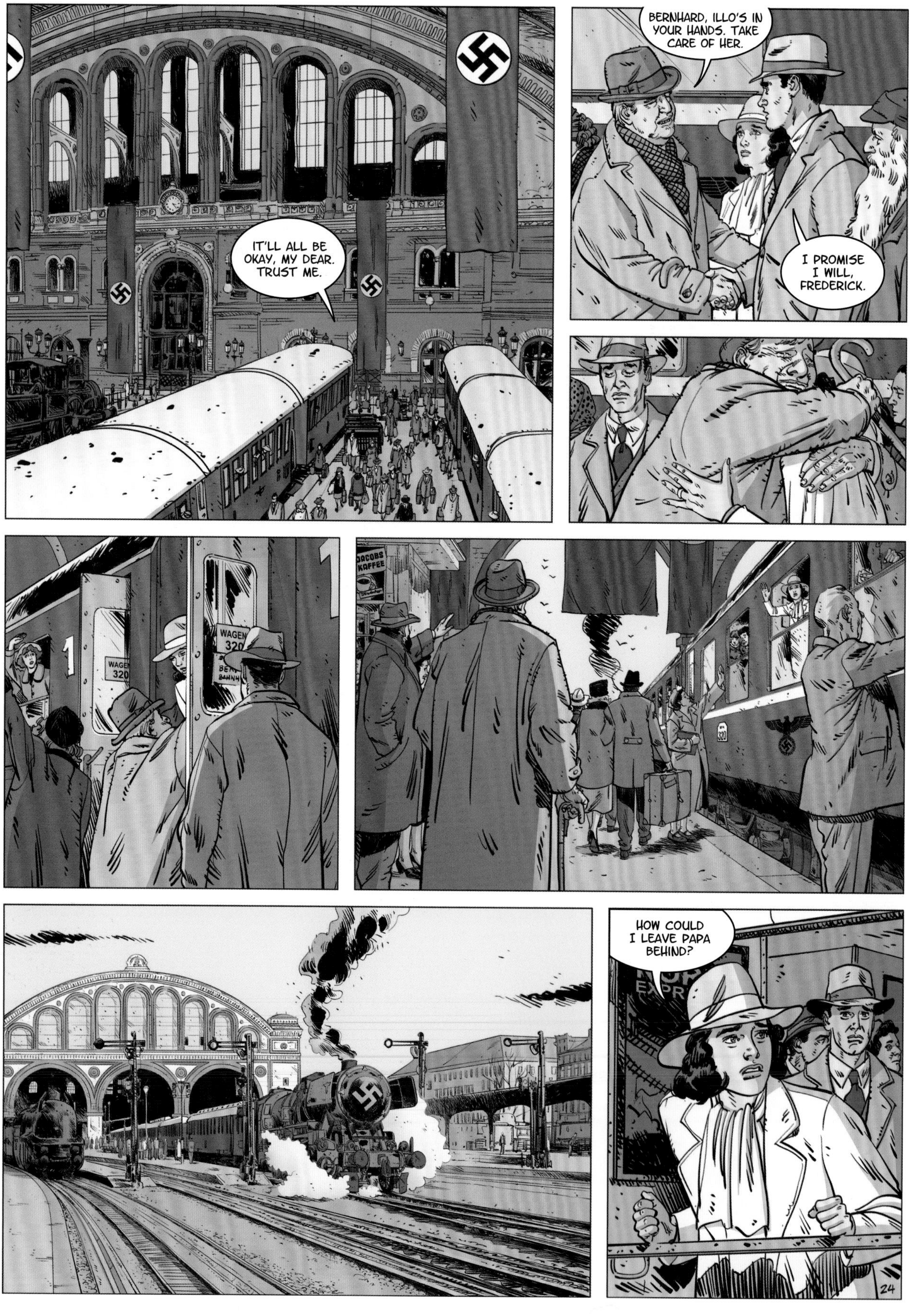
IT'LL ALL BE OKAY, MY DEAR. TRUST ME.
BERNHARD, ILLO'S IN YOUR HANDS. TAKE CARE OF HER.
I PROMISE I WILL, FREDERICK.
WAGEN 320
WAGEN 320
JACOBS KAFFEE
HOW COULD I LEAVE PAPA BEHIND?
24

TWO HOURS LATER...

BERNHARD... IF WE EVER GOT SEPARATED, WOULD YOU STILL FILM MY SCRIPT?

OF COURSE! BUT WHY IMAGINE THE WORST? WE'RE TOGETHER, YOU AND ME, AND THAT'S HOW WE'LL STAY!

TRAIN LEAVES IN 15 MINUTES!

I SUPPOSE I SHOULD MAKE THE MOST OF IT. I'M GOING TO RUN TO THE STATION RESTROOM.

I LOVE YOU.

LOVE YOU, TOO. BE QUICK!

HEY, THIS SEAT IS TAKEN!

SO WHY'S IT EMPTY, THEN?

MOVE THAT CASE OR I'LL THROW IT OUT THE WINDOW!

YOU WOULDN'T BE ABLE TO LIFT IT.

TRAIN DEPARTING!

WHERE'S ILLO?

BERNHARD! HERE I AM!

I WAS SO AFRAID! NEVER DO THAT TO ME AGAIN.

25

WHY ARE YOU IN HERE?

OPEN THIS SAFE!

MONEY, OK, BUT WHERE'S YOUR GOLD?

I HAVEN'T HAD ANY FOR A LONG TIME, AS MENTIONED IN MY DECLARATION.

AND NOW, GET OUT OF MY ESTABLISHMENT!

YOU JEWS ARE LIARS AND THIEVES. "YOUR" ESTABLISHMENT, AS YOU PUT IT, NO LONGER BELONGS TO YOU. BY DECREE OF NOVEMBER 12TH, 1938, ALL JEWS WITHOUT EXCEPTION ARE TO BE EXCLUDED FROM GERMAN ECONOMIC LIFE. YOUR PROPERTY HAS BEEN REQUISITIONED FOR THE REICH. SO, YOU WILL GET OUT, THIS INSTANT!

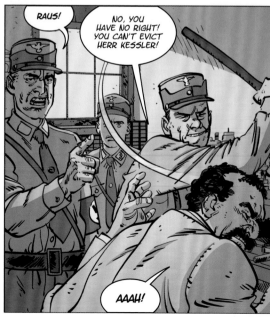

RAUS!

NO, YOU HAVE NO RIGHT! YOU CAN'T EVICT HERR KESSLER!

AAAH!

COME, EZER. IT ISN'T WORTH IT. PLEASE PICK UP MY MEDALS AND LET'S GO.

I'M AFRAID TODAY, WE'VE BEEN BEAT...

BRENNER STATION, ON THE REICH'S ITALIAN BORDER...

DO YOU HAVE MORE THAN TEN REICHSMARKS ON YOU, OR ANY UNAUTHORIZED JEWELRY THAT ISN'T IN THE INVENTORY?

N-NO... IT'S ALL DECLARED.

SEARCH HIM!

NO, MATTHIAS! TELL THEM THE TRUTH!

IT'S THE END OF THE LINE FOR THOSE DISHONEST JEWS. ARE YOU NAUGHTY JEWS, TOO?

EVERY-THING'S IN ORDER.

THE SEALS AREN'T BROKEN.

MOVE ON, THEN.

NEXT!

PORT OF GENOA, ITALY...

FOLLOW ME TO YOUR CABIN, PLEASE.

POTSDAM

GENOVA

YOU MUST VISIT THE CASHIER TO RECEIVE YOUR TOKENS. BON VOYAGE!

AH, YES, OUR TOKENS...

WELL, NOW! THAT AWFUL WOMAN FROM THE TRAVEL AGENCY MIGHT HAVE BEEN RIGHT AFTER ALL.

IT'S ALMOST AS IF WE'RE OFF ON OUR HONEYMOON!

EXCEPT WE WON'T BE GOING HOME AT THE END.

"THINKING OF YOUR FATHER?"

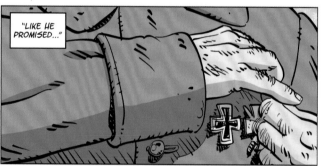

"LIKE HE PROMISED..."

"IT WILL BE ALRIGHT."

28

30

WHY ARE YOU HERE?

I'M HERE TO ASK YOU TO LEAVE MY PREMISES.

YOU'RE A STUBBORN KIKE. I AM THE LAW, YET YOU INSULT IT.

YOUR SINFUL LAWS MEAN NOTHING!

HELP! HELP!

BANG BANG

FILTHY RABBLE!

29

LOOK AT YOU... I MUST BE THE LUCKIEST GUY IN THE WORLD.

ATTENTION... ATTENTION... THE SHIP WILL BE SAILING IN 15 MINUTES!

LET'S GO UP ON DECK! WOULDN'T WANT TO MISS THE DEPARTURE. LEAVE THE SUITCASES! COME ON!

I NEED A FEW MINUTES. GO AHEAD, I'LL JOIN YOU.

YOU AGAIN?

WHAT, YOU GONNA THROW ME OVERBOARD?

BERNHARD HERSCH, I'M TRAVELING WITH MY WIFE, ILLO.

WE'RE HEADING TO SHANGHAI TO BEGIN WITH, THEN WE'LL EMIGRATE TO THE U.S.

SHLOMO BLUEM. I'M GOING TO JAPAN TO JOIN MY WIFE AND KIDS... THEY WENT FIRST. I'LL BE GETTING OFF IN KOBE.

YOUR WIFE'S MISSIN' ONE HELL OF A SHOW, BERNHARD!

30

ILLO?

WHERE IS SHE?!

"MY LOVE, I JUST CAN'T BRING MYSELF TO ABANDON MY FATHER. DESPITE WHAT HE SAYS, HE'S WEAK... BUT YOU ARE STRONG."

"WE'LL BOTH JOIN YOU SOON, I SWEAR IT. YOU'LL BE A BRILLIANT TRAILBLAZER FOR US, I KNOW YOU WILL."

ILLO!

"I BEG YOU TO WAIT FOR ME AND NEVER GIVE UP ON OUR DREAM. IF WE BOTH SET OUR MINDS TO IT, THEN WE'LL NEVER BE TRULY APART."

ILLO?

WHAT ARE YOU DOING? SWIMMING BACK TO PORT? YOU'RE CRAZY!

SHE... SHE DID THE CRAZIEST THING IMAGINABLE!

31

SHLOMO? WHY ARE YOU UNDER THERE INSTEAD OF IN YOUR CABIN?

I GOT ARRESTED ON *KRISTALLNACHT** AND SENT TO ORANIENBURG CAMP FOR A MONTH, INCLUDING 23 DAYS IN SOLITARY CONFINEMENT WITH NO LIGHT AND HARDLY ANY AIR. MY CABIN'S GOT NO PORTHOLE. IT'S TOO STUFFY. I CAN'T STAND IT.

I CAN'T TAKE ANY MORE OF THIS, BERNHARD! I HAVEN'T SEEN MY FAMILY IN TWO-AND-A-HALF YEARS. THERE'S A BIG JEWISH COMMUNITY IN KOBE 'N I KNOW MY WIFE 'N DAUGHTERS ARE OK...I JUST MISS THEM SO MUCH.

I UNDERSTAND... BUT REMEMBER, IT'S JUST SIX SHORT WEEKS TILL YOU SEE THEM AGAIN.

I HOPE SO...

ALL IN GOOD TIME. LET'S DEAL WITH YOUR CABIN PROBLEM FIRST.

HOW?

MINE HAS A PORTHOLE AND ONE SPARE BERTH.

HEY... SORRY FOR COMPLAININ'.

AND THANKS, FRIEND.

*"THE NIGHT OF BROKEN GLASS": A POGROM AGAINST JEWS PERPETRATED BY NAZI GERMANY IN BERLIN ON NOVEMBER 9TH AND 10TH, 1938. OVER A HUNDRED JEWS DIED AND 30,000 WERE DEPORTED TO CONCENTRATION CAMPS.

BERLIN...

WHAT HAPPENED?

IT'S CLOSED. GET OUT!

OH, FRÄULEIN ILLO...

THE NAZIS KILLED HIM.

PLEASE, FRÄULEIN ILLO! DON'T DO ANYTHING FOOLISH! IT WON'T BRING HERR KESSLER BACK TO US.

MURDERERS!

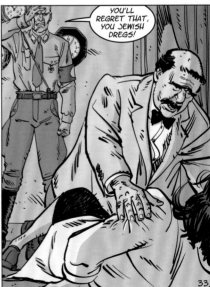

YOU'LL REGRET THAT, YOU JEWISH DREGS!

33

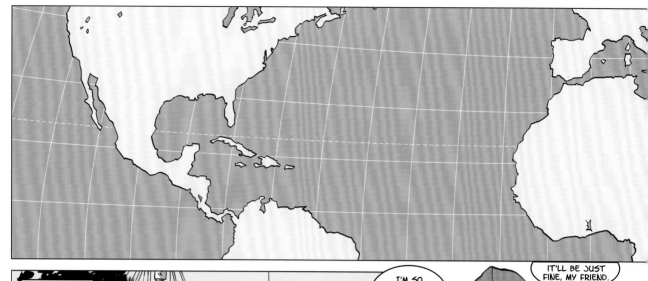

KOBE, JAPAN...

I'M SO NERVOUS. I'M SHAKIN' LIKE A LEAF.

IT'LL BE JUST FINE, MY FRIEND.

THERE THEY ARE, BERNHARD! ALL OF 'EM! OH, LORD ALMIGHTY!

YOUR VISA IS INVALID.

W-WHAT? IT IS VALID, I SWEAR! WITH ALL THE NECESSARY STAMPS!

IT'S PERFECTLY VALID!

YOU CANNOT DISEMBARK IN JAPAN. NEXT!

34

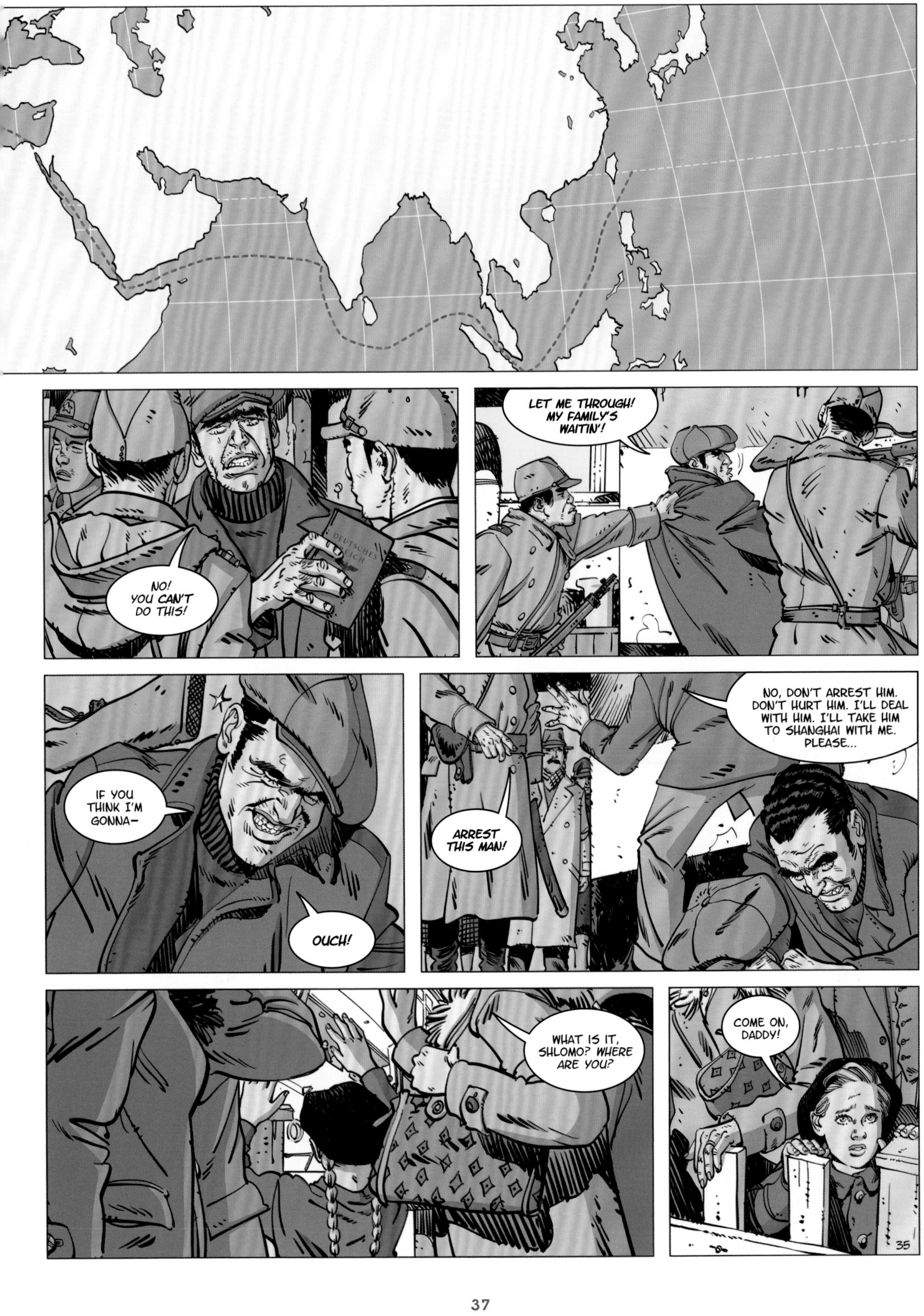

DEUTSCHES
NO! YOU CAN'T DO THIS!
LET ME THROUGH! MY FAMILY'S WAITIN'!
IF YOU THINK I'M GONNA-
OUCH!
ARREST THIS MAN!
NO, DON'T ARREST HIM. DON'T HURT HIM. I'LL DEAL WITH HIM. I'LL TAKE HIM TO SHANGHAI WITH ME. PLEASE...
WHAT IS IT, SHLOMO? WHERE ARE YOU?
COME ON, DADDY!
35

THE EAST CHINA SEA...

THAT'S IT! HERE WE ARE IN SHANGHAI!

YES, IT'S SHANGHAI!

HOW FANTASTIC!

HURRAY!

AND HERE I WAS, EXPECTING TO FIND A PUTRID RATHOLE!

WHAT DIFFERENCE DOES IT MAKE IF WE CAN'T BE WITH OUR FAMILIES?

36

BUT... WE'RE GOING PAST THE OLD CITY...

WHERE ARE WE HEADED?

DON'T TELL ME WE'RE GOING TO ANCHOR HERE?!

POTSDAM

A PUTRID RATHOLE... YOU MUST BE PSYCHIC, BERNHARD.

BUT I PROBABLY WOULDA ADDED "WAR-TORN"...

CHARITY! GIVE ME!

RICKSHAW, MILORD! RICKSHAW!

GIVE MONEY!

WHO DO THEY THINK WE ARE? RICH KIDS OFF ON A WORLD TOUR?

LADIES AND GENTLE-MEN! I AM ABRAHAM EISENMAN OF THE JDC...

JOINT! WE'RE SAFE, THEN!

IS THIS SOME MISTAKE? WE WON'T BE LIVING HERE, WILL WE, MR. EISENMAN?

RELAX. A BUS WILL MAKE SEVERAL TRIPS TO TAKE YOU TO ONE OF JOINT'S HOSTELS. THE PHILANTHROPIST MAURY KAUFMAN OWNS AN OFFICE BUILDING ON SEWARD ROAD AND HE'S SET AN ENTIRE FLOOR OF IT ASIDE FOR REFUGEES.

BUT BEFORE YOU MOVE IN THERE, YOU NEED TO HAVE AN URGENT MEDICAL CHECKUP AND GET VACCINATED.

HERE WE ARE: THE CLINIC. EVERYBODY OUT OF THE TRUCK NOW, PLEASE.

YOU MUSTN'T FORGET TO BOW TO ANY JAPANESE SOLDIERS YOU MIGHT MEET, EVEN LOW-RANKING SENTRIES. OTHERWISE YOU'LL GET INTO SERIOUS TROUBLE AND I WON'T BE ABLE TO HELP YOU OUT.

38

YOU WILL BE GIVEN WATER. UNDER *NO CIRCUMSTANCES* SHOULD YOU USE IT UNLESS IT'S BEEN BOILED FIRST, EVEN FOR BRUSHING YOUR TEETH.

AND YOU MUSTN'T EAT UNCOOKED FRUIT OR VEGETABLES, EITHER.

OPEN WIDE!

NEXT!

MR. EISENMAN, HOW CAN I GO ABOUT CONTACTING BERLIN? IS THERE A TELEPHONE AT THE *HEIM**?

COMMUNICATION FACILITIES ARE ALMOST NON-EXISTENT HERE. A FEW MINUTES ON THE TELEPHONE WOULD COST YOU A MONTH'S SALARY... IF YOU EVEN MANAGED TO GET A LINE, THAT IS. IT'S SIMPLER AND SAFER TO SEND A LETTER VIA JOINT.

*TEMPORARY JEWISH HOUSING COMPLEX IN SHANGHAI.

OH, GREAT! AN OFFICE REFITTED AS A DORMITORY...

IT'LL GET US IN THE MOOD TO FIND A JOB. EISENMAN SAYS WE CAN RENT ROOMS IN FAMILY GUESTHOUSES IN THE CHINESE DISTRICT OF HONGKOU, BUT IT'S EXPENSIVE WITHOUT A DECENT SALARY.

I HOPE MY LETTER REACHES ILLO...

♪ "BY THE WAYSIDE STANDS..." ♪

BERLIN...

♪ "...A BENT TREE." ♪

♪ "ALL ITS BIRDS HAVE FLOWN AWAY." ♪

40

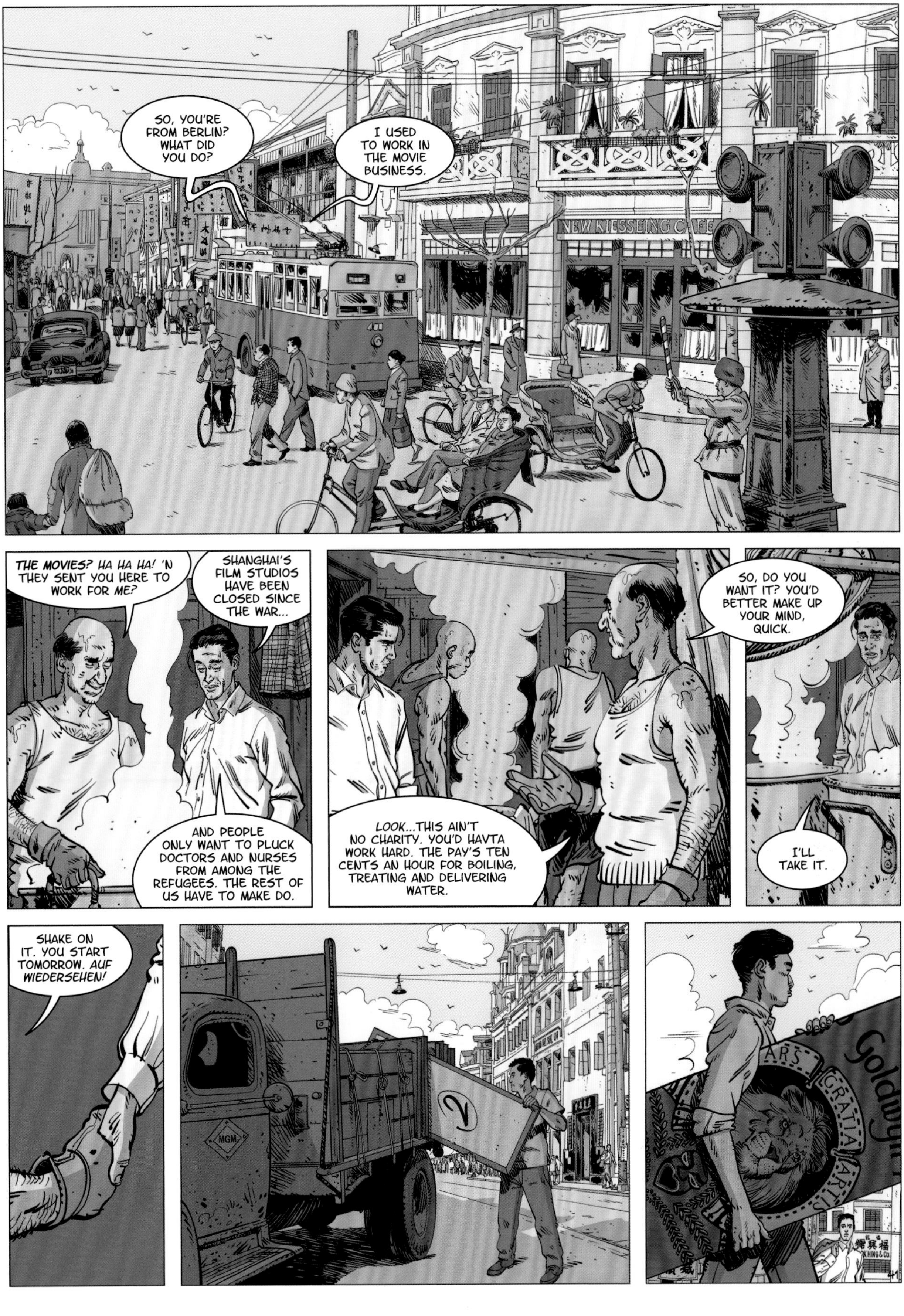
SO, YOU'RE FROM BERLIN? WHAT DID YOU DO?
I USED TO WORK IN THE MOVIE BUSINESS.
NEW KIESSEING CAFE
THE MOVIES? HA HA HA! 'N THEY SENT YOU HERE TO WORK FOR ME?
SHANGHAI'S FILM STUDIOS HAVE BEEN CLOSED SINCE THE WAR...
AND PEOPLE ONLY WANT TO PLUCK DOCTORS AND NURSES FROM AMONG THE REFUGEES. THE REST OF US HAVE TO MAKE DO.
LOOK...THIS AIN'T NO CHARITY. YOU'D HAVTA WORK HARD. THE PAY'S TEN CENTS AN HOUR FOR BOILING, TREATING AND DELIVERING WATER.
SO, DO YOU WANT IT? YOU'D BETTER MAKE UP YOUR MIND, QUICK.
I'LL TAKE IT.
SHAKE ON IT. YOU START TOMORROW. AUF WIEDERSEHEN!
MGM
Goldwyn
ARS GRATIA ARTIS

HEY, WAIT!

EXCUSE ME, SIR. DO YOU SPEAK ENGLISH? CAN YOU TELL ME WHAT THIS PLACE IS?

I CAN. THESE ARE MGM SHANGHAI'S NEW OFFICES. THE OLD ONES WERE DAMAGED IN THE LAST TYPHOON.

WELL, CHENG? WHEN WILL MY NEW GODDAMN DESK GET HERE?

TOMORROW, MR. HANOVER.

DID YOU ORDER THE BIG ONE?

THE BIGGEST, MR. HANOVER. SOLID MAHOGANY.

OK, I'M LEAVIN'. LEMME KNOW WHEN WE CAN START WORKIN'.

AND THAT WOULD BE MY BOSS...

42

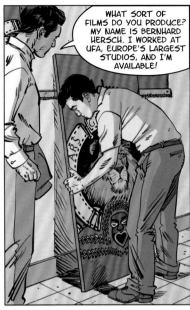

WHAT SORT OF FILMS DO YOU PRODUCE? MY NAME IS BERNHARD HERSCH. I WORKED AT UFA, EUROPE'S LARGEST STUDIOS, AND I'M AVAILABLE!

OK, THAT MEANS YOU WORKED FOR THE NAZIS...

NEVER! I LOATHE THE NAZIS! IT'S BECAUSE OF THEM THAT I'M HERE, THOUSANDS OF MILES AWAY FROM MY HOME AND ALL MY LOVED ONES!

THAT'S MORE LIKE IT. WE CHINESE HAVE OUR OWN NAZIS: CRUEL BRUTES, MURDERERS AND MONSTERS, JUST LIKE THEM. THEY'RE CALLED JAPANESE...

I SYMPATHIZE WITH YOU, MR. HERSCH, BUT MGM SHANGHAI ISN'T ACTUALLY INVOLVED IN PRODUCTION. IT ONLY DISTRIBUTES AMERICAN MOVIES.

AND NO MOVIES ARE MADE IN SHANGHAI ANY MORE. ALL THE PRODUCERS, TECHNICIANS AND BIG-SCREEN STARS HAVE FLED TO HONG KONG.

TRADE

BUT STILL, I WISH YOU THE BEST OF LUCK.

WAIT!

WAIT! HIRE ME! GIVE ME ANY OLD JOB. I CAN DO ANYTHING! I KNOW ALL ABOUT THE MOVIE BUSINESS AND AMERICAN CINEMA... I PROMISE I'D BE VERY USEFUL.

MGM SHANGHAI IS TWO PEOPLE: ME AND MR. HANOVER. I CARRY ALL THE REELS AND POSTERS MYSELF. I'M VERY SORRY BUT, AGAIN, I HAVE NOTHING TO OFFER YOU.

43

FIVE MONTHS LATER, IN 1939...

CAN YOU BELIEVE MY WIFE *STILL* DOESN'T WANNA LEAVE KOBE?

IT'S TRUE... SHE 'N THE KIDS HAVE SETTLED IN WELL OVER THERE. SHE DOESN'T WANNA COME TO SHANGHAI JUST FOR OUR FAMILY TO LIVE IN POVERTY.

'N NOW YOU'RE LEAVIN'...

I'M SORRY, MY FRIEND.

HOW WILL YOU BE ABLE TO AFFORD YOUR NEW LODGINGS? YOUR WAGES 'N WHAT I EARN AT MY PEANUT-CRUSHING FACTORY AREN'T ENOUGH FOR A ROOM IN A CHINESE GUESTHOUSE.

I HAVE A SCHEME, BUT I COULDN'T PASS ON THE TIP, EVEN IF I WANTED TO...

AND ILLO?

I'M REALLY WORRIED. SHE HASN'T REPLIED TO ANY OF MY LETTERS. IN DESPERATION, I WROTE TO AN OLD FRIEND WHO'S CLOSE TO THE NAZIS TODAY. HIS POSITION MIGHT ALLOW HIM TO GET NEWS OF ILLO.

I'M SURE SHE'S DOING ALL SHE CAN TO COME AND JOIN YOU. SHE'S PROBABLY ON HER WAY ALREADY! WHEN SHE SHOWS UP, WHAT AM I SUPPOSED TO TELL HER? THAT YOU RAN OFF BECAUSE YOU COULDN'T TAKE ANY MORE OF OL' SHLOMO?

אדאנק*
SHLOMO.

ניטא פאר וואָס**
BERNHARD.

*"ADANK" (THANK YOU) AND **"NITA FAR VAS" (YOU'RE WELCOME) ARE BOTH TRANSLATED FROM YIDDISH.

BERLIN...

HERE IS YOUR MAIL, HERR STRAUSS.

A LETTER FROM SHANGHAI?

BERNHARD HERSCH...

Bernhard Hersch Jewish Joint SHANGHAI

Herr MANFRED UFA studio Berlin-Deut

MANFRED! MINISTER GOEBBELS AND LENI RIEFENSTAHL ARE COMING!

I'M READY TO RECEIVE THEM, BUT RUDOLF...

YES, WHAT IS IT?

CAN I SEE YOU AFTER THE VISIT? I HAVE A FAVOR TO ASK...

HEIL HITLER!

45

47

YOU DIDN'T *BOW* FOR A PASSING PATROL!

YOU'LL PAY FOR THAT, YOU *SUBHUMAN*!

OUT OF THE WAY, CHANKORO MUTTS!

THAT'S THE LAST WE'LL SEE OF *HIM...*

ROOM UPSTAIRS.

GREAT, MR. WONG. I'LL FOLLOW YOU.

亚麻纱亚麻纱、马术表演的纸房

ROOM IS OK?

HMM... YES, FINE.

LIN LIN. DAUGHTER.

IF NEED, YOU ASK HER.

MAY I MAKE YOUR BED NOW, SIR? THE WONG HOUSEHOLD IS ENTIRELY AT YOUR DISPOSAL AND EAGER TO PLEASE YOU.

47

COMPLIMENTS ON YOUR ENGLISH, MISS. YES, PLEASE MAKE THE BED.

MY WIFE WILL JOIN ME. WE'LL NEED ANOTHER BED.

Wilde Nacht in Berlin

... WE'VE ONLY BEEN APART FOR A SHORT WHILE, BUT IT FEELS LIKE AN ETERNITY...

I DO HOPE SHE COMES TO SHANGHAI SOON, SIR.

DO YOU HAVE ANY NEWS FROM HER? IS SHE ALRIGHT?

MAKE HER UP A BEAUTIFUL BED WITH SCENTED SHEETS. THAT'LL BRING HER BACK SOONER...

...I HOPE.

48

ILLO, I SWEAR THAT WHEN YOU JOIN ME IN SHANGHAI, WE'LL LEAVE THIS HELL SOMEHOW AND GET TO HOLLYWOOD. I'LL DIRECT YOUR SCRIPT. WE'LL MAKE OUR FILM TOGETHER.

"WE'VE ONLY BEEN APART FOR A SHORT WHILE, BUT IT FEELS LIKE AN ETERNITY."

EMMA JUST CAME INTO AN INHERITANCE. SHE'D LIKE TO STAY LONGER IN NEW YORK BUT HER FATHER BOUGHT HER A RETURN TICKET AND SHE DOESN'T HAVE TIME TO LINGER IN THE CITY."

"HER TRAIN LEAVES IN TWENTY MINUTES—JUST LONG ENOUGH TO GET TO THE STATION. SHE GLANCES INTO A SHOP WINDOW..."

"...AND SEES A DRESS – THE DRESS."

"AT THAT MOMENT, FRANK PASSES BY THE SHOP AND SEES A WOMAN—THE WOMAN."

"CUT!"

49

SEPTEMBER 1, 1939...

IS BERNHARD HERSCH AROUND?

SHLOMO! HOW ARE YOU? STILL DOWN AT THE PEANUT FACTORY?

SURE THING. WHY WOULD I QUIT MY DREAM JOB?

THIS CAME FOR YOU AT THE HEIM.

IS IT ILLO AT LAST?

Telegramm

Deutsche Reichspost

21-08-1939- UFA STUDIOS- BERLIN =

NEUIGKEITEN VON ILLO

Berlin

VON RUDOLF MEI

BERNHARD?

SEHR SCHLECHTE NEUIGKEITEN

ILLO VERHAFTET UND IM ARBEITSLAG

50

ILLO ARRESTED THEN SENT TO LABOR CAMP

ELISA!

ILLO TREATED BY RAVENSBURK DOCTORS

LEAVE HER! MOVE!

I CAN CARRY HER! IF SHE STAYS HERE, SHE WON'T WAKE UP! PLEASE! LET ME!

LEAVE HER! NOW!

BUT DIED OF TYPHUS

BLAM!

SINCEREST CONDOLENCES

51

THIS IS IT! IT'S REALLY OVER!

BERNHARD! AYE, WAIT! CALM DOWN! IT'S GONNA BE ALRIGHT!

NO-O-O-O!

LADIES AND GENTLEMEN! MY NAME IS ABRAHAM EISENMAN. PLEASE FOLLOW ME TO A BUS THAT WILL TAKE YOU TO ONE OF JOINT'S HEIMS...

BUT NO... NO... NO!

SHE'S NOT DEAD. SHE WAS RELEASED. SHE'S COMING. SHE'S HERE! ILLO, I'M HERE! ILLO!

I'VE WAITED FOR YOU, MY LOVE! HERE I AM!

ILLO...

ILLO!

TWO MONTHS LATER...

SO MANY CLOTHES...

ARE YOU REALLY GOING TO KEEP THEM ALL?

THEY'RE ALL I HAVE LEFT OF ILLO.

SHE HAD EXCELLENT TASTE.

DON'T YOU TOUCH THAT!

I... I'M SORRY...

I'M THE ONE WHO'S SORRY FOR YOU, BERNHARD.

WAIT, I TRULY AM SORRY...

IF YOU'LL LET ME EXPLAIN...

THERE IS NOTHING TO EXPLAIN.

I WILL MEND THIS... GOOD AS NEW.

PLEASE PULL YOURSELF TOGETHER, BERNHARD. I REALLY HATE TO SEE YOU LIKE THIS.

THANKS FOR BEING SO KIND, LIN LIN... YOU HAVE NO IDEA WHAT IT MEANS TO ME...

I HEAR HER VOICE... AT NIGHT... SHE COMES TO ME IN MY DREAMS-- SHE HAD NO RIGHT TO LEAVE ME LIKE THAT... I NEVER SAW IT COMING, YOU UNDERSTAND?

2

NOW LOOK WHAT YOU'VE DONE!

I SHOULD HAVE STOPPED HER FROM GOING BACK THERE. IT'S MY FAULT THAT SHE'S DEAD.

MY FAULT!

BE GENTLE WITH THEM!

SORRY, I'M ACTING LIKE A MONSTER... CAN YOU REPAIR IT?

AND WHAT ARE ALL THESE?

NOTHING.

OH, EXCUSE ME... WILL YOU SHOUT AT ME AGAIN IF I TOUCH THEM?

DID IT ALSO BELONG TO YOUR WIFE?

YES.

A MOVIE SCRIPT?

YES.

WOULD YOU CARE TO TELL ME ABOUT IT?

WE INVESTED A LOT OF OURSELVES INTO THIS PROJECT. ILLO WROTE IT; I WAS TO DIRECT. A BEAUTIFUL DREAM...

LIN LIN, PLEASE DON'T BE OFFENDED, BUT COULD I ASK YOU TO LEAVE ME ALONE WITH MY MEMORIES FOR A WHILE?

FINE, BUT DO TRY TO COME DOWNSTAIRS AND EAT A LITTLE.

OH, ILLO... ILLO.

HEY, WHAT IS THIS THING?!

I'M TERRIBLY SORRY, SIR.

BUT... ILLO, WAIT! IT'S ME, BERNHARD...

I DON'T KNOW YOU. LEAVE ME ALONE.

WHAT ARE YOU PLAYING AT?! I'M YOUR HUSBAND!

5

YOU'RE CONFUSING ME WITH SOMEONE ELSE! PLEASE, I NEED TO GET OFF THIS TRAIN!

AND YOUR FUNERAL WREATH?

WAIT... WAIT... THIS IS YOURS!

SORRY, BERNHARD, BUT I JUST CAN'T STAY.

HALT!

NO, ILLO! PLEASE DON'T GO WITH THEM! COME BACK!

ILLO! ILLO!

ILLO...

GRAND THEATRE CINEMA, SHANGHAI INTERNATIONAL SETTLEMENT...

THEY HAVE STRUCK! DISREGARDING ITS PROMISES AND WORLD PUBLIC OPINION, GERMANY HAS INVADED POLAND.

THE POLISH PEOPLE HAVE SEEN THEIR TOWNS DESTROYED, THEIR MEN MURDERED OR THROWN IN PRISON.

OWING TO THIS INTOLERABLE AGGRESSION, ENGLAND AND FRANCE HAVE NOW DECLARED WAR ON GERMA--

AT LEAST THIS NEW JOB ALLOWS ME TO REREAD ILLO'S SCRIPT IN PEACE...

SSSHHHLACK!

SCHEIBE!

?!

HOOOFF!

I... I DON'T UNDERSTAND!

...AND I NEVER WANNA SEE YOU AGAIN! GOT IT?!

7

IMPERIAL JAPANESE NAVY HQ, SHANGHAI...

CAPTAIN INUZUKA, I ASK FOR YOUR SUPPORT.

OFFICE OF CAPTAIN KORESHIGE INUZUKA, HEAD OF THE BUREAU ON JEWISH AFFAIRS, SHANGHAI...

YOU WON'T REGRET THIS, I CAN ASSURE YOU.

A REQUEST FOR PERMISSION TO OPEN A NEW FILM STUDIO...

I WANT TO REVIVE CINEMA IN SHANGHAI AND MAKE BEAUTIFUL, IMPORTANT FILMS.

MAKE MOVIES HERE, IN SHANGHAI? I SHALL LOOK INTO IT, MR. KAUFMAN. I HAVE HAD NO CAUSE TO REGRET TRUSTING YOU THUS FAR.

I HAVE ALWAYS BELIEVED THAT ALLOWING JEWISH BUSINESS TO DEVELOP WOULD BE PROFITABLE FOR JAPAN.

MY SUPERIORS HAVE HONORED ME BY LISTENING.

I IMAGINE YOUR NAZI ALLIES ARE LESS ENTHUSIASTIC, CAPTAIN.

62

MY IDOL IS JOE DIMAGGIO, MR. KAUFMAN.

DIMAGGIO NEVER CARED ABOUT BEING LIKED, ONLY WINNING.

I BOUGHT THIS GLOVE, WHICH WAS REPUTED TO HAVE BELONGED TO THE CHAMPION, THOUGH I DOUBT IT.

SINCE YOU'RE HERE, I TAKE IT YOU'D LIKE US TO WIN THIS MATCH TOGETHER, MR. KAUFMAN?

AH, HERE COMES THE SAKE.

SERVE US, LIN LIN, THEN GO.

YOU MENTIONED THE NAZIS, MR. KAUFMAN, BUT THEY ARE FAR AWAY. IN SHANGHAI, IT IS I WHO DECIDES EVERYTHING THAT CONCERNS THE JEWS AND THEIR BUSINESSES.

SO, LET'S DRINK TO BUSINESS AND BASEBALL: OUR TWO PASSIONS!

KANPAI!

LIN LIN? WHAT ARE YOU DOING?

CLEANING! I...I WAS THINKING ABOUT ILLO'S SCRIPT. I'D LIKE TO READ IT.

IN GERMAN?

THAT'S TRUE... PITY. ARE YOU STILL WORKING ON IT?

I'M GOING TO FILM IT. I'M NOT SURE HOW I'LL MANAGE YET. I DON'T SPEAK CHINESE AND ALL THE STUDIOS HAVE CLOSED DOWN, BUT I HAVE TO DO IT. I SIMPLY *MUST*... THIS IS ALL I'VE GOT LEFT...

I MIGHT HAVE AN IDEA...

10

THIS IS A GREAT HONOR FOR ME, MR. KAUFMAN.

YOUR FRIEND LIN LIN KNOWS ALL ABOUT MY AMBITIONS.

MR. HERSCH ALREADY WORKS FOR YOU, MR. KAUFMAN, AT THE GRAND THEATRE.

WELL, I USED TO. I... I'M FREE TO DEVOTE MYSELF TO MY FILM FROM NOW ON.

I LIKE THE PLOT, BUT UNFORTUNATELY, THE SCRIPT'S IN GERMAN AND IT'S SET IN BERLIN! WHAT AM I SUPPOSED TO DO WITH THAT?

I WON'T EVEN BOTHER ASKING YOU FOR AN ENGLISH TRANSLATION SO WE CAN READ IT...

WHAT IF I TRANSFERRED THE WHOLE STORY TO SHANGHAI?

WITH CHINESE ACTORS?

UH, WELL, I...

IF YOU DO ALL THAT, THEN I PROMISE I'LL READ IT. BUT DON'T GET YOUR HOPES UP TOO HIGH, MR. HERSCH!

I'M SORRY, BUT WE GAVE IT A TRY.

DON'T BE SORRY. WE'LL MAKE THE FILM, EVEN IF I HAVE TO STAND OUTSIDE KAUFMAN'S OFFICE, DAY AND NIGHT!

I NEVER SHOULD HAVE MENTIONED IT. NOW YOU'LL BE EVEN MORE UPSET THAN BEFORE.

NOT AT ALL. IT'S A GOOD THING YOU DID!

YOUR AUNT BEQUEATHED YOU SOME MONEY. USE IT *WISELY*, AND GIVE MY BEST REGARDS TO YOUR PARENTS.

IT'S SO GORGEOUS, BUT I COULD NEVER WEAR IT...

YOU *WON'T* MISS YOUR TRAIN, I PROMISE! LET ME DRIVE YOU...

13

♪ WHEN I LOOK INTO YOUR EYES ♪ NOTHIN' BUT BLUE SKIES 'N BUTTERFLIES ♪

KNOCK
KNOCK

COME IN.

I'VE READ THE BEGINNING! I LIKE IT!

...ILLO WAS INCREDIBLY TALENTED.

MAY I READ THE REST?

"I'M STILL DOING THE ENGLISH TRANSLATION. IT TAKES TIME... WHAT DID YOU THINK SO FAR?"

OF COURSE. I UNDERSTAND.

THE STORY REMINDS ME OF ONE OF MY FAVORITE COMEDIES: EDMUND GOULDING'S GRAND HOTEL, WITH GRETA GARBO... IT'S ALSO SET IN BERLIN.

AND DID YOU LIKE HOW I'VE TRANSFERRED IT TO SHANGHAI?

WELL... THE HEROINE WOULD NEVER TAKE A TRAIN WITH A FUNERAL WREATH...

IN CHINA, THE PILLOW UPON WHICH THE DEAD RESTED THEIR HEAD MUST BE DESTROYED.

"THE PILLOW IS THROWN ONTO THE ROOF OF THE DEAD PERSON'S HOUSE, TO ROT AWAY AND DISAPPEAR."

"SO, YOUR HEROINE, JIA LI, THROWS HER AUNT'S PILLOW, BUT..."

UH-- BUT ONLY IF YOU AGREE... PERHAPS IT'S TOO BIG A CHANGE? THERE'D BE NO TRAIN ANYMORE...

THAT DEPENDS WHETHER IT'S SET IN THE COUNTRY, AND IF THERE'S A LITTLE STATION...

YOU COULD MAKE IT YUHANG REGION! THAT'S ABOUT 120 MILES AWAY FROM SHANGHAI.

SO, THE PILLOW RISES, THEN FALLS...

"...BUT NOT ON THE ROOF!"

"JIA LI IS TERRIBLY EMBARRASSED."

WHAT D'YOU SAY?

IT SOUNDS PRETTY GOOD TO ME...

GOSH, SORRY. I... EXCUSE MY MANNERS...

NO, I'M VERY GLAD TO SEE IT, AFTER SO MANY WEEKS...

YOU'RE EATING AGAIN-- AND WHAT AN APPETITE!

WHY ARE YOU HELPING ME LIKE THIS, LIN LIN?

YOU KNOW... I COULD NEVER FORGET ABOUT ILLO. NO ONE COULD EVER TAKE HER PLACE...

I KNOW WHAT IT MEANS TO LOSE A LOVED ONE... I LOST MY PARENTS...

WH...WHAT HAPPENED TO THEM? I'VE BEEN GOING ON ABOUT ILLO FOR MONTHS, I NEVER EVEN ASKED TO HEAR YOUR STORY...

I THOUGHT THE OWNERS OF THE GUESTHOUSE--

NO, THEY'RE NOT MY PARENTS. THEY'RE MY COUSINS. THEY TOOK ME IN AFTER MY PARENTS WERE MASSACRED.

"MASSACRED?"

"YES, BY THE JAPANESE IN NANKING."

"IT'S A CITY 180 MILES FROM SHANGHAI. TWO YEARS AGO, THE JAPANESE CAPTURED NANKING AND SLAUGHTERED HUNDREDS OF THOUSANDS OF SOLDIERS AND CIVILIANS."

"MY PARENTS AND I WERE HIDING AMONG ALL THE CORPSES..."

"...PLAYING DEAD..."

"BUT IF THE JAPANESE *START* A JOB, THEY LIKE TO *FINISH* IT."

"I HAVE NOTHING LEFT THAT BELONGED TO MY PARENTS. I WISH I COULD'VE KEPT SOMETHING OF THEIRS..."

LIKE THE WAY YOU'VE KEPT ILLO'S SCREENPLAY.

LIN LIN, I... I'M SO SORRY.

IF ILLO'S SCRIPT EVER GETS MADE INTO A MOVIE, IT'LL BE A BIT LIKE THE CHILD WE COULD'VE HAD, THE TWO OF US...

17

DECEMBER 1941...

HELLO, SHLOMO!

BERNHARD!

WHAT'S THIS?! YOU'RE SO DRESSED-UP! TELL ME ALL ABOUT IT!

I'VE BEEN LIVING IN HONGKOU FOR LONG ENOUGH. I KNOW LOTS OF PEOPLE, I CAN FIND YOU SOME DECENT LODGINGS! THIS PLACE--

NO, NO. I WANNA SAVE UP EVERY LAST CENT FOR MY GIRLS.

BUT, WHY?

18

BLUMA'S REFUSIN' TO LEAVE THE JEWISH COMMUNITY IN KOBE... 'N SINCE YOU, ME, 'N ALL THESE REFUGEES AIN'T ALLOWED TO EMIGRATE...

IN THE END, BLUMA'S RIGHT. WHAT CAN I GIVE 'EM BUT THIS SHOND KHAY*?

BUT IT'S BREAKIN' MY HEART.

*"SHAME OF A LIFE" IN YIDDISH.

THE JAPANESE JUST BOMBED THE PORT OF PEARL HARBOR!

WHAT'S THAT YOU SAY?!

A NAVAL BASE IN HAWAII... THE JAPANESE AIR FORCE... THEY ATTACKED IT! SANK SOME SHIPS, KILLED AMERICAN SOLDIERS...

THIS TIME THE AMERICANS WILL DEFINITELY ENTER THE WAR.

EXCUSE ME, SHLOMO. I NEED TO GO SEE SOMEONE URGENTLY. I'LL BE BACK.

*"SHAME OF A LIFE" IN YIDDISH.

I'M HERE TO SEE MR. KAUFMAN.

MR. HERSCH, GIVEN THE LATEST EVENTS, MR. KAUFMAN IS MUCH TOO BUSY TO SEE YOU NOW.

HE RECEIVES A LARGE NUMBER OF REQUESTS--

SHANGHAI DREAM

SAVE YOUR BREATH! I GET THE PICTURE, BUT I'M WARNING YOU: I'M NOT BUDGING UNTIL MR. KAUFMAN TELLS ME "NO" HIMSELF, STRAIGHT TO MY FACE.

WHY SO FORMAL?! CALL ME MAURY!

AH, THE SHANGHAI DREAMER! PLEASE, LET'S GO AND SIT DOWN.

FORGIVE DALBERT. HE'S JUST DOING HIS JOB.

SO, YOU'VE FINALLY READ IT?

YES, AND I'VE SENT IT TO BE TRANSLATED INTO CHINESE. IT'S JUST THE KIND OF STORY I NEED TO GET THE NEW STUDIO UP AND RUNNING1

AND THE CHERRY ON TOP: YOU HAVE EXPERIENCE DIRECTING!

LET'S JUST SAY I KNOW HOW THINGS WORK IN A STUDIO...

WHAT ABOUT PEARL HARBOR-- THE AMERICANS... WON'T THAT PUT US IN JEOPARDY?

'COURSE NOT! WHATEVER MAKES YOU THINK THAT?

NEVERMIND...

I WON'T LET YOU DOWN, MR. KAUFMAN!

I BELIEVE YOU. WE NEED SOME YOUNG BLOOD, NEW TALENT, FRESH IDEAS...

AH, HERE'S THE STUDIO DIRECTOR, MR. CHENG.

HELLO, MR. CHENG. I'M LOOKING FORWARD TO WORKING WITH YOU.

PLEASE BERNHARD, CALL ME MENG.

I KNOW EXACTLY WHAT YOU NEED, MR. KAUFMAN, AND FOR THAT, WE'LL NEED YOUR MONEY, RIGHT BERNHARD?

HA! HA! HA! THE FAR EAST FILM COMPANY'S BUDGET WILL BE GENEROUS, I PROMISE YOU! I WANT OUR PRODUCTIONS TO BE LAVISH!

FAR EAST FILM COMPANY

LIN LIN!

THANK YOU! YOU MADE ALL OF THIS POSSIBLE!

C'MON! LET'S GO CELE-BRATE THIS AMAZING NEWS IN THE FRENCH QUARTER! WHAT DO YOU SAY?

BERNHARD, I JUST CAN'T... MY COUSINS WOULD WONDER WHERE ON EARTH I WAS DASHING OFF TO LIKE THAT... AND WITH A WESTERNER...

COME UP TO MY ROOM.

WHY NOT COME OUT WITH ME IN THIS DRESS YOU SEEMED TO LIKE SO MUCH? HERE! IT'S YOUR SIZE! YOU COULD PASS FOR A WESTERN GIRL...

WHAT ARE YOU DOING?

ILLO'S DRESS? YOUR WIFE'S DRESS?!

WHAT? WHAT DID I SAY?

SLAM!

WE'LL BE SHOOTING *IN HERE?!* AFTER ALL THIS TIME, COULDN'T KAUFMAN HAVE FOUND SOMETHING *BETTER* THAN THIS OLD *WAREHOUSE?* HONESTLY...

M. KAUFMAN STUDIOS

AH, MENG! I'VE DRAWN UP THE SCHEDULE. TAKE A LOOK! I'VE SPENT *WEEKS* GOING OVER ALL THE DETAILS TO MAKE SURE IT WAS READY.

EXCELLENT! BUT FIRST, ALLOW ME TO INTRODUCE THE TECHNICAL CREW.

Opening September 1st
M. KAUFMAN PRESENTS

KAUFMAN PRESENTS

BERNHARD, PLEASE MEET YOUR TEAM: CHU-WAI LEUNG, OUR CAMERAMAN; YU-SEN WU, SOUNDMAN; SING-LUNG CHAN, DIRECTOR OF PHOTOGRAPHY; AND YU-TUNG CHENG, HIS ASSISTANT.

AND THIS IS LIANG-YONG WU, OUR ART DIRECTOR.

BUT-- WHERE ARE ALL THE OTHERS? WHERE ARE MY ASSISTANTS?

WE ARE *FAR* FROM BERLIN... LET ALONE HOLLYWOOD, BERNHARD! KAUFMAN'S GIVING US NEXT TO NOTHING. WE MUST BE RESOURCEFUL.

BUT WE CAN MAKE IT.

ALRIGHT THEN.

UH... WHO SPEAKS ENGLISH?

23

SEVERAL DAYS LATER...

SILENCE! WE'RE STARTING THE AUDITIONS FOR JIA LI AND BAO-TIAN.

THIS IS THE SCENE WHERE THEY FIRST MEET. JIA LI, IN AN EVENING DRESS, IS RUNNING TO THE STATION TO CATCH A TRAIN, BUT BAO-TIAN CHASES HER, PLYING HER WITH QUESTIONS. JIA LI HAS A HARD TIME GETTING RID OF HIM. FIRST COUPLE, STEP FORWARD...

SEVERAL HOURS LATER...

NO, STOP! STOP!

停止！

I CAN'T BELIEVE THIS! THIS COUPLE IS THE LAST STRAW! THEY'RE GLOWERING AT EACH OTHER!

PERHAPS IT LOOKS WRONG TO YOU BECAUSE OF THE LANGUAGE BARRIER, BERNHARD...

BUT, PLEASE, TRUST ME--THEY CAN DO IT.

OK, THEN... LET'S START WITH THE BASICS...

M. KAUFMAN STUDIOS

THE SCRIPT.

SCRIPT.

SCRIPT.

THE CAMERA.

CAMERA.

THE MIC.

MIC.

AND THIS IS THE C--

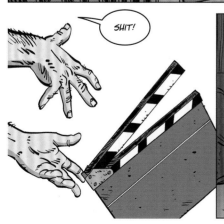

SHIT!

SHIT.

25

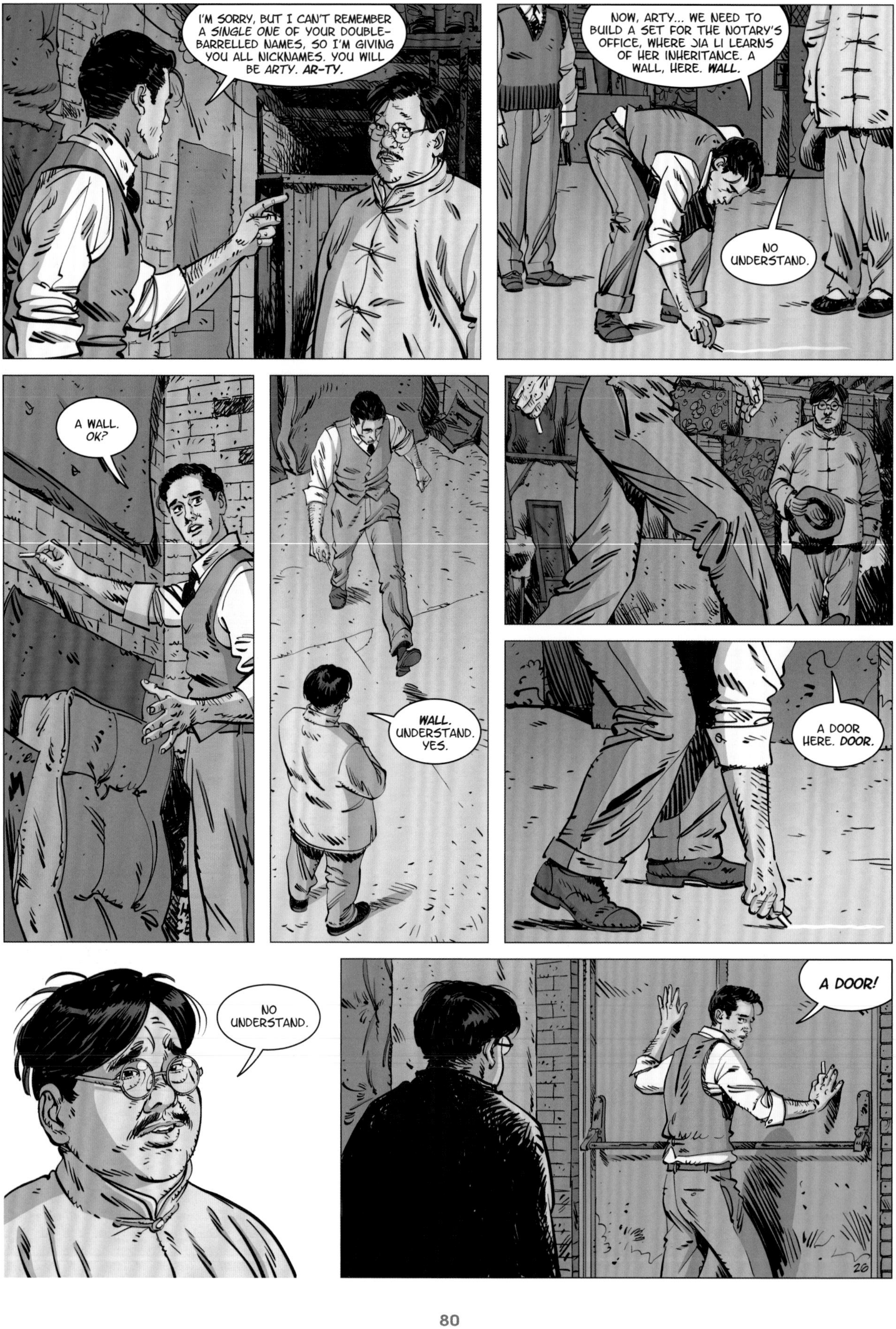
I'M SORRY, BUT I CAN'T REMEMBER A *SINGLE* ONE OF YOUR DOUBLE-BARRELLED NAMES, SO I'M GIVING YOU ALL NICKNAMES. YOU WILL BE *ARTY*. ***AR-TY.***
NOW, ARTY... WE NEED TO BUILD A SET FOR THE NOTARY'S OFFICE, WHERE JIA LI LEARNS OF HER INHERITANCE. A WALL, HERE. ***WALL.***
NO UNDERSTAND.
A WALL. *OK?*
WALL. UNDERSTAND. YES.
A DOOR HERE. ***DOOR.***
NO UNDERSTAND.
A DOOR!
26

MAYBE I *WAS* TOO HASTY ABOUT JIA LI AND BAO-TIAN...? WE CAN HOLD ANOTHER AUDITION AND RE-CAST THE COUPLE...

NO, YOU WERE RIGHT. THEY'RE THE ONES.

YOU THOUGHT THEY WERE *AWFUL!* AND ANOTHER THING: THOSE TWO ARE IN LOVE, BUT THEY KEEP BREAKING UP. ONE OF THEM MIGHT *DITCH* US...

I WANT *THEM* TO PLAY JIA LI AND BAO-TIAN, AND *NOBODY* ELSE.

LOOK... WE'RE GOING TO NEED EXTRA HANDS TO BUILD THE SETS. I'D LIKE AN INTERPRETER, BUT SHE'LL HAVE TO BE PAID. KAUFMAN HAD BETTER START REACHING INTO HIS POCKETS, OR THIS WILL BE A DISASTER. COME, LET ME SHOW YOU...

THE SET FOR THE SHANGHAI NOTARY'S OFFICE... WHAT DO YOU THINK?

OF *THAT?* UH-- WHAT IS IT, EXACTLY?

WHY DON'T YOU ASK OUR ART DIRECTOR... ARTY, COME HERE, PLEASE! CAN YOU TELL MR. CHENG WHAT THAT IS SUPPOSED TO BE?

A DOOR!

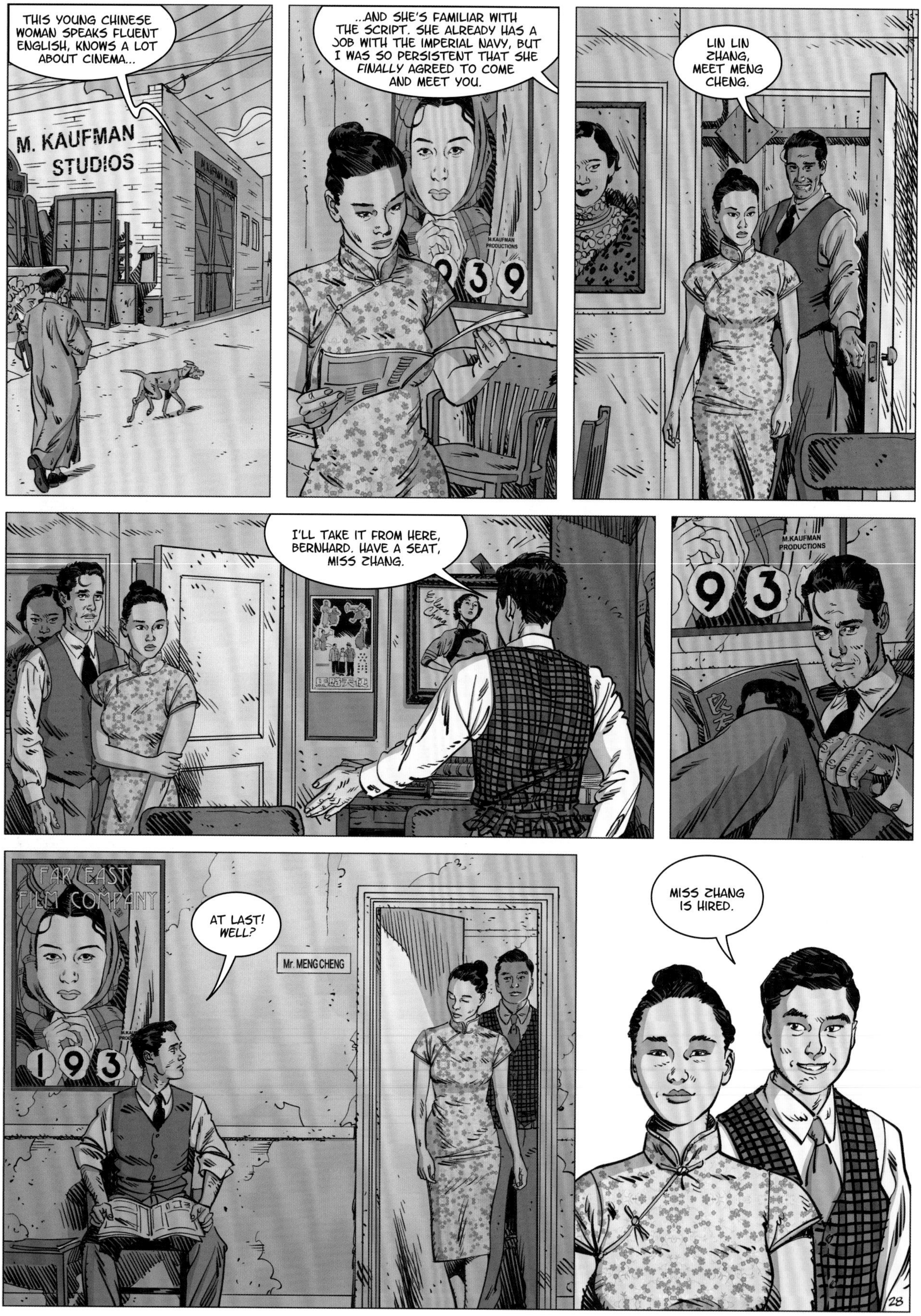
THIS YOUNG CHINESE WOMAN SPEAKS FLUENT ENGLISH, KNOWS A LOT ABOUT CINEMA...
M. KAUFMAN STUDIOS
...AND SHE'S FAMILIAR WITH THE SCRIPT. SHE ALREADY HAS A JOB WITH THE IMPERIAL NAVY, BUT I WAS SO PERSISTENT THAT SHE *FINALLY* AGREED TO COME AND MEET YOU.
M.KAUFMAN PRODUCTIONS
939
LIN LIN ZHANG, MEET MENG CHENG.
I'LL TAKE IT FROM HERE, BERNHARD. HAVE A SEAT, MISS ZHANG.
M.KAUFMAN PRODUCTIONS
93
FAR EAST FILM COMPANY
193
AT LAST! WELL?
Mr. MENG CHENG
MISS ZHANG IS HIRED.
28

SHLOMO! I'M MAKING A MOVIE AND I NEED YOUR HELP. COME WITH ME TO THE STUDIO!

WHAT DO I GOTTA DO?

EVERYTHING! YOU'LL BE PAINTING SETS AT FIRST--

SHLOMO! GUESS WHO'S HERE!

BLUMA! MY GIRLS!

THEY'VE MISSED YOU SO MUCH!

AND SO HAVE I!

YOU KNOW ALL I CAN OFFER YOU IS THIS SHOND KHAY...

WITH YOU, WE'LL NEVER BE ASHAMED OF ANYTHING!

29

TELL SHU WEI THAT THIS IS WHEN THE NOTARY EXPLAINS EXACTLY HOW MUCH SHE'S INHERITED, AND SHE'S ASTOUNDED.

LAMPY, IS THE LIGHT OK?

好的, 先生

CAMY?

ALL GOOD, SOUNDY?

SHANGHAI DREA

SCENE 7 TAKE 1

BERNHAR

CAMERA!

ACTION!

CUT! THAT'S A WRAP!

BRAVO, BERNHARD! THIS'LL BE A GREAT MOVIE!

YES, IT WILL, MAURY... THANKS TO YOU.

THREE WEEKS LATER...

HALT!

OH, I'M SO SORRY!

MY CAP... JUST TAKING IT OFF... PLEASE ACCEPT MY APOLOGIES.

I'M RUNNING LATE FOR WORK TODAY. THAT'S WHY I DIDN'T--

CAMY'S BEEN ARRESTED!

HE'S BEING HELD AT THE JAPANESE MILITARY POLICE BUILDING.

FINDING A REPLACEMENT WILL BE TOUGH AT SUCH SHORT NOTICE.

CAMY IS PART OF MY CREW. I'LL GO GET HIM OUT!

HE'S GONE TO FREE CHU-WAI!

OH!

HEADQUARTERS OF THE TOKKEITAI, JAPANESE NAVAL MILITARY POLICE...

CAPTAIN, MY NAME IS BERNHARD HERSCH.

KAUFMAN, THE JEW?

I AM A MOVIE DIRECTOR, WORKING FOR MR. MAURY KAUFMAN'S STUDIO, THE FAR EAST FILM COMPANY.

31

MY CAMERAMAN, CHU-WAI LEUNG, GOT ARRESTED BY THE JAPANESE MILITARY POLICE THIS MORNING. WITHOUT HIM, MY ENTIRE SHOOT WILL FALL APART.

HERE'S A LIST OF THE NAMES AND ADDRESSES OF MY WHOLE CREW, ALONG WITH ALL THE NECESSARY PERMITS, INCLUDING THIS ONE, SIGNED BY CAPTAIN INUZUKA HIMSELF.

YOUR CHINAMAN FAILED TO REMOVE HIS CAP FOR SOME JAPANESE SOLDIERS--A VERY SERIOUS CRIME. I MUST TURN HIM OVER TO THE KENPEITAI*.

WOULD YOU PLEASE TELL ME WHAT EXACTLY YOU ARE DOING?

MAY I HUMBLY OFFER TO PAY HIS FINE, CAPTAIN, THUS PUNISHING HIM OFFICIALLY FOR HIS MISDEMEANOR AND ALLOWING YOU TO RELEASE HIM FROM YOUR CUSTODY?

THIS IS GOLD. YOU CAN CHECK.

LOOK WHAT THOSE BASTARDS HAVE DONE TO YOU!

PROCESS THIS LIST, LIEUTENANT!

*THE IMPERIAL JAPANESE ARMY'S MILITARY POLICE, EQUIVALENT TO THE GESTAPO.

32

THE NEXT DAY...

CAPTAIN NAKANO, MY TECHNICIANS AND LEADING ACTORS HAVE BEEN ARRESTED! THIS IS TOTALLY ARBITRARY AND *UNFAIR!*

INTO MY OFFICE, HERSCH.

YOU MUST PAY THE DETAINEES' FINES IN FULL, OR THEY WILL BE SENT TO BRIDGE HOUSE*.

THIS IS ALL I'VE GOT.

NOW, PLEASE LET ME FINISH MAKING MY MOVIE...

33

*THE KENPEITAI HEADQUARTERS IN SHANGHAI.

FOLLIES A SELLY GOD FELA, FOLLIES A SELLY GOD FELA!

WHEN THEY WERE MAKING *THE CABINET OF DR. CALIGARI,* THEY WERE ALSO PLAGUED BY POWER CUTS, SO THE DIRECTOR HAD THE SETS PAINTED ACCORDING TO THE TYPE OF LIGHT HE WANTED AT A PARTICULAR TIME OF DAY.

SHLOMO! GO AND BRING ALL THE LEFTOVER PAINT YOU CAN FIND!

I THINK SO. IT'S ALL CLEAR. I KNOW THE FILM.

WE NEED TO CREATE ILLUSIONS THAT GIVE THE EFFECT OF MORNING LIGHT OR NIGHT LIGHT. DO YOU THINK YOU'LL BE ABLE TO EXPLAIN THAT TO THEM?

KAUFMAN STUDIOS

ON TIME TOMORROW, OK CAMY?

ON TIME, SIR!

IT'S A WONDER WE'RE NOT EVEN FURTHER BEHIND SCHEDULE.

IT'S ALL THANKS TO YOUR ENERGY AND MOTIVATION. ILLO WOULD BE PROUD OF YOU.

YES, LIN LIN. I KNOW, TOMORROW'S THURSDAY. I KNOW YOUR SCHEDULE AND EVERYONE ELSE'S AROUND HERE. WE'LL GET BY SOMEHOW...

BERNHARD, I'M NOT COMING TOMORROW. I'LL BE WORKING FOR CAPTAIN INUZUKA... BERNHARD... DID YOU HEAR ME?

FINE, THEN! SINCE YOU KNOW HOW TO DO EVERYTHING BETTER THAN ANYONE ELSE, YOU CAN DO IT *WITHOUT ME!*

LIN LIN! WHAT'S GOTTEN INTO HER?

IS IT WOMEN I CAN'T UNDERSTAND OR JUST CHINESE WOMEN?

35

HELLO, BERNHARD!

HELLO, BLUMA.

COME ON IN, BUDDY! IT'S ALWAYS GREAT HAVIN' YOU FOR SHABBAT.

WE'LL NEVER BE ABLE TO THANK YOU ENOUGH FOR FINDING US THIS HOME.

COME, BERNHARD! THE GIRLS ARE OUT BACK.

SHARNA! EIDEL! GO HELP YOUR MOTHER.

YEAH, WE'RE HAPPY HERE--AS MUCH AS WE CAN BE. WE'RE ALL BACK TOGETHER AS A FAMILY AGAIN...BUT I'M STILL WORRIED, Y'KNOW.

THOSE DAMN NAZIS HAVE FORCED THE JAPANESE INTO PASSIN' A LAW TO MAKE ALL THE JEWS IN SHANGHAI REGISTER WITH THE POLICE.

PLEASE TELL ME THE NIGHTMARE AIN'T GONNA START UP AGAIN HERE, BERNHARD.

I HAVE NO IDEA, SHLOMO... SO WHY DON'T WE GO MAKE THE MOST OF THIS NICE RESPITE THE ALMIGHTY HAS GRANTED US?!

TOKKEITAI HEADQUARTERS, JANUARY 1943...

GERMANY IS CURRENTLY DEALING WITH THE JEWISH QUESTION IN EUROPE. YOU'VE ALLOWED TOO MANY REFUGEES INTO SHANGHAI: OVER TWENTY THOUSAND JEWS ALREADY! THEY OUGHT TO BE DEPORTED TO POLAND!

YOU HAVE JUST ARRIVED, COLONEL MESSINGER. YOU WILL SEE FOR YOURSELF THAT THERE IS NO "JEWISH QUESTION" HERE IN SHANGHAI.

THEY RUN LARGE BUSINESSES, HOTELS, MOVIE THEATERS, RADIO STATIONS AND NEWSPAPERS, ALL TO SPREAD THEIR POISON! THERE ARE THOUSANDS OF THEM, AND THEY'RE BREEDING LIKE DAMN RATS!

I ASK THAT YOU NOT RAISE YOUR VOICE AT ME IN FRONT OF MY MEN.

YOUR MEN! THEY AGREE WITH ME...

GENTLEMEN, THIS MEETING IS OVER...

THE FÜHRER WILL BE ANGRY.

I DO NOT TAKE ORDERS FROM YOUR FÜHRER.

NOT YET...

OFFICE OF THE MILITARY GOVERNOR...

THANK YOU FOR THE REPORT, CAPTAIN INUZUKA. I SHALL PASS IT ON TO TOKYO.

BUT, BEFORE THAT, I WISH TO ELUCIDATE A MATTER WHICH REMAINS A MYSTERY TO ME, AND I THINK YOU CAN HELP.

THE NEXT DAY...

GENERAL, THIS IS THE VENERABLE RABBI SHIMON SHOLOM KALISH, A SCHOLAR AND WISE MAN WHO SHOULD BE ABLE TO ENLIGHTEN YOU. WHAT WAS YOUR QUESTION?

WHY DO THE NAZIS HATE THE JEWS SO MUCH?

ZUGIM WEIL MIR SENEN ORIENTALIM.

THE NAZIS HATE US BECAUSE WE ARE ORIENTAL. THEY ARE TALL AND BLONDE, AND THEY HATE ALL SHORT, DARK-HAIRED FOLK...

DO YOU UNDERSTAND, GENERAL?

ABSOLUTELY.

GOOD. INUZUKA. YOU MAY LEAVE.

38

FINALLY...! IT'S OUR LAST DAY ON SET FOR *SHANGHAI DREAM!* WE'LL BE SHOOTING THE MOST CRUCIAL SCENES! HELL, I CAN HARDLY BELIEVE IT!

WHERE'S LIN LIN, MRS. WONG? I CAN'T FIND HER.

AT MR. KAUFMAN'S.

LOAN SHARK RACK
PROMISE TO PAY

M. KAUFMAN STUDIOS

WHAT? CLOSED UNTIL FURTHER NOTICE DUE TO *JEWISH* OWNERSHIP!

LOOK! IT CAN'T BE! THIS IS A NIGHTMARE!

'N STARTIN' TOMORROW, JEWS ARE NO LONGER PERMITTED TO WORK ANYWHERE OUTSIDE OF HONGKOU.

WHAT?! NO, THAT'S IMPOSSIBLE! NOT SO CLOSE TO THE END OF THE SHOOT!

COOL DOWN, BERNHARD! THIS IS MORE SERIOUS THAN MOVIES!

ALL THOSE PEOPLE CRAMMED INTO THE GHETTO WITH NOTHIN' AT ALL! THINK WHAT'LL BECOME'A THEM!

M. KAUFMAN STUDIOS

YOU DON'T GET IT! I HAVE TO FINISH THIS MOVIE! I *HAVE* TO DO IT, FOR ILLO!

NO, NO, NO... THIS IS NOT HAPPENING! MAURY WILL FIX IT!

AND WHO'S THIS BUNCH COMIN' NOW?

THE KENPEITAI!

TEARING UP AN OFFICIAL NOTICE IS VERY SERIOUS.

40

YOU ARE UNDER ARREST!

YOU'RE ON THE PROPERTY OF MAURY KAUFMAN!

IT'S TRUE. THIS IS A MISTAKE-- THOSE REGULATIONS DON'T APPLY TO US!

ISN'T MAURY KAUFMAN A JEW?

AND AREN'T YOU JEWISH, TOO?

NO, MENG! DON'T EVEN TRY IT!

BLAM!

ALL ENEMIES OF JAPAN MUST DIE.

BE CAREFUL WITH ALL MY POSSESSIONS!

SHANGHAI TRANSPORTATION.Co

I'M LETTING GO OF SO MANY TREASURES. SUCH A TRAGEDY...

AND WHAT CAN I DO FOR YOU, MISS ZHANG?

THE JAPANESE EXECUTED MENG CHENG, MR. KAUFMAN, AND BERNHARD HERSCH HAS BEEN ARRESTED BY THE KENPEITAI. THERE'S NO TELLING WHAT THEY'LL DO TO HIM.

CAPTAIN INUZUKA IS YOUR FRIEND. HE'S WELL CONNECTED... I'M BEGGING YOU TO DO SOMETHING...

NOTHING I CAN DO, MISS. HERSCH KNOWS THAT THE KENPEITAI WILL ALWAYS FIND YOU GUILTY...

WRAP THAT ONE UP CAREFULLY, NOW!

PLEASE... YOU MUST DO SOMETHING FOR HIM!

I WAS WRONG TO GET INTO THIS BUSINESS AT ALL. I LOST A PILE OF MONEY, AND NOW MY LIFE AND MY FAMILY ARE BEING THREATENED...

IF THAT'S WHY YOU'RE LEAVING, THEN FINE--GO! BUT WHY WOULD YOU WANT TO LOSE EVEN MORE MONEY?

WHAT'S THIS?

THE ONLY WAY TO NOT LOSE ALL YOUR MONEY IS TO FINISH THE FILM, AND FOR THAT, YOU HAVE TO GET THE DIRECTOR RELEASED.

DON'T TELL ME THERE ISN'T SOME LAST STRING YOU CAN PULL THAT COULD POSSIBLY SAVE HIS LIFE!

... PERHAPS THERE IS A WAY...

I JUST HOPE IT'S NOT PACKED DEEP INSIDE THE TRUCK YET.

STOP! OPEN THAT UP!

GIVE THIS TO CAPTAIN INUZUKA. IT'LL WORK MAGIC FOR HERSCH. IT'S PRICELESS!

43

TOKKEITAI HEADQUARTERS...

ENOUGH! AAAH! ENOUGH! NO-O-O!

STOP!!! AAAH!

THAT WILL DO FOR TODAY. TAKE HIM BACK TO HIS CELL.

STOP IT... STOP...

HERSCH! GET UP!

NO, ENOUGH! I'M BEGGING YOU, NOT AGAIN...

YOU HAVE VISITOR!

LIN LIN?!

YOU, HERE... A MIRACLE... NO, I'M DREAMING...

YES, A MIRACLE... OR, RATHER, VISITING RIGHTS SIGNED BY...

...JOE DIMAGGIO!

45

THE SOLDIERS WILL ONLY GIVE ME A FEW MINUTES, SO I'LL MAKE IT QUICK: THEY'VE REDUCED YOUR SENTENCE TO LIFE IMPRISONMENT.

"LIFE" IN HERE WOULD BE ABOUT THREE WEEKS BEFORE CROAKING...

NO-- YOU'RE TO BE TRANSFERRED TO A PRISON CAMP. YOU'LL BE FAR FROM THE KENPEITAI'S CLUTCHES.

BUT, YOU'RE STILL GOING TO NEED PLENTY OF COURAGE.

I DON'T KNOW. I CAN'T PROMISE ANYTHING, LIN LIN. WITHOUT MY FILM, I'LL HAVE NOTHING BUT PAIN AND HEARTBREAK...

COME ON, YOU CAN GET THROUGH THIS. YOU MUST RESIST. YOU HAVE TO LIVE! YOU WILL GET OUT. YOU HAVE A REASON: I'LL BE HERE WAITING FOR YOU, BERNHARD! YOU'RE NOT ALONE.

VISITING TIME UP!

THANKS, LIN LIN... I'M NOT QUITE SURE WHAT TO MAKE OF THAT. I'VE TOLD YOU, NO ONE CAN REPLACE ILLO, BUT THANK YOU... IT MEANS A LOT TO ME.

WHAT I MEANT WAS, UNLESS YOU INTEND TO USE YOUR TIME IN PRISON TO LEARN CHINESE, YOU'RE GOING TO NEED ME IF YOU WANT TO FINISH YOUR FILM...

46

YANGCHOW INTERNMENT CAMP, JULY 17, 1945. MORE THAN TWO YEARS LATER...

BBBBRRRRRRRRRRRRRRRRR

WHAT A NOISE! SOUNDS LIKE A WHOLE SQUADRON!

THE AMERICANS! THEY'VE COME TO KICK THESE JAPS' ASSES! THEY'RE SCREWED NOW!

アメ公だ!

THEY'RE GONNA BOMB SHANGHAI!

WE'RE GONNA BE FREE!

47

MEI VERY WORRIED. OUR GUEST VERY DIFFERENT.

HE'S BEEN BACK FOR SIX MONTHS, BUT I CAN STILL BARELY RECOGNIZE HIM... WE HAVE TO KEEP HOPING--

TAKE ME THERE. PLEASE, LIN LIN. IT'S TIME!

I DIDN'T WANT TO BRING YOU BACK.

I WAS AFRAID IT WOULD ONLY MAKE YOU FEEL WORSE...

M KAUFMAN

THE STUDIO IS STILL STANDING.

DO YOU REALLY WANT THE ROOF OF THIS DECREPIT OLD BUILDING TO CAVE IN ON OUR HEADS?

YOU CAN HELP ME MAKE SOME PHONE CALLS...

48

SEVERAL WEEKS LATER...

WELL, NOW, WHAT D'YOU SAY TO THAT?

SHANGHAI

WOW. YOU ALL CAME...

THANK YOU, MR. KAUFMAN.

YOU'VE MADE SOME SACRIFICES TO GET US ALL BACK HERE-- ME IN PARTICULAR.

MISS ZHANG CAN BE QUITE PERSUASIVE.

I'M NOT AS WELL-OFF AS I WAS BEFORE THE WAR, BUT I STILL HAVE ENOUGH CASH TUCKED AWAY TO MAKE SURE SHANGHAI DREAM DOESN'T STAY A DREAM.

Opening
September 1st
M. KAUFMAN
PRESENTS

SO... SHALL WE FINISH THIS MOVIE?

CAMERA!

ACTION!

SHANGHAI DREAM
FINAL SCENE

49

SHANGHAI
DREAM
上海梦

COMING SOON TO A
THEATER NEAR YOU

ILLO...

1772

LIN LIN,
CLIMB ABOARD
THE TRAIN.

上海
SHANGHAI

上海
SHANGHAI
上海

WHEN IT STARTS TO
MOVE OFF, STAND AT
THE WINDOW IN THE
COMPARTMENT.

THEN WE SEE BAO-TIAN
RUN DOWN THE PLAT-
FORM TOWARDS HIS
TRUE LOVE...

...HIS TRUE
LOVE, JIA LI--
THAT'S YOU.
ALL CLEAR?

ILLO! WHAT
ARE YOU
DOING?

50

上海
SHANGHÁI

LIN LIN IS SUPPOSED TO--

NO, BERNHARD. I'M THE ONE BOARDING THIS TRAIN.

I'M GOING, BERNHARD. ALONE.

YOU HAVE TO LET ME GO, MY LOVE. FROM NOW ON, THIS BELONGS TO YOU. FAREWELL!

51

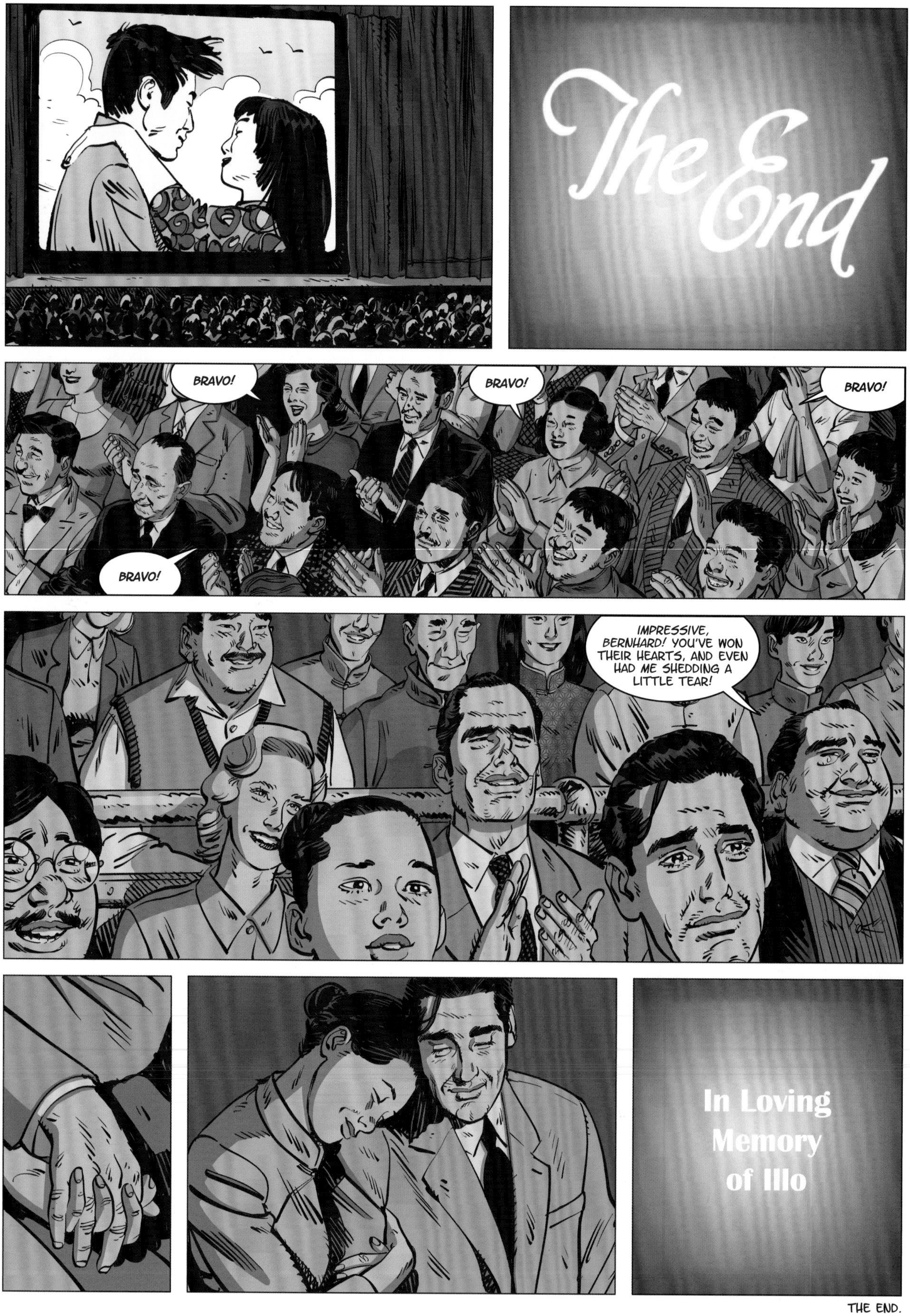
The End
BRAVO!
BRAVO!
BRAVO!
BRAVO!
IMPRESSIVE, BERNHARD! YOU'VE WON THEIR HEARTS, AND EVEN HAD ME SHEDDING A LITTLE TEAR!
In Loving Memory of Illo

THE END.

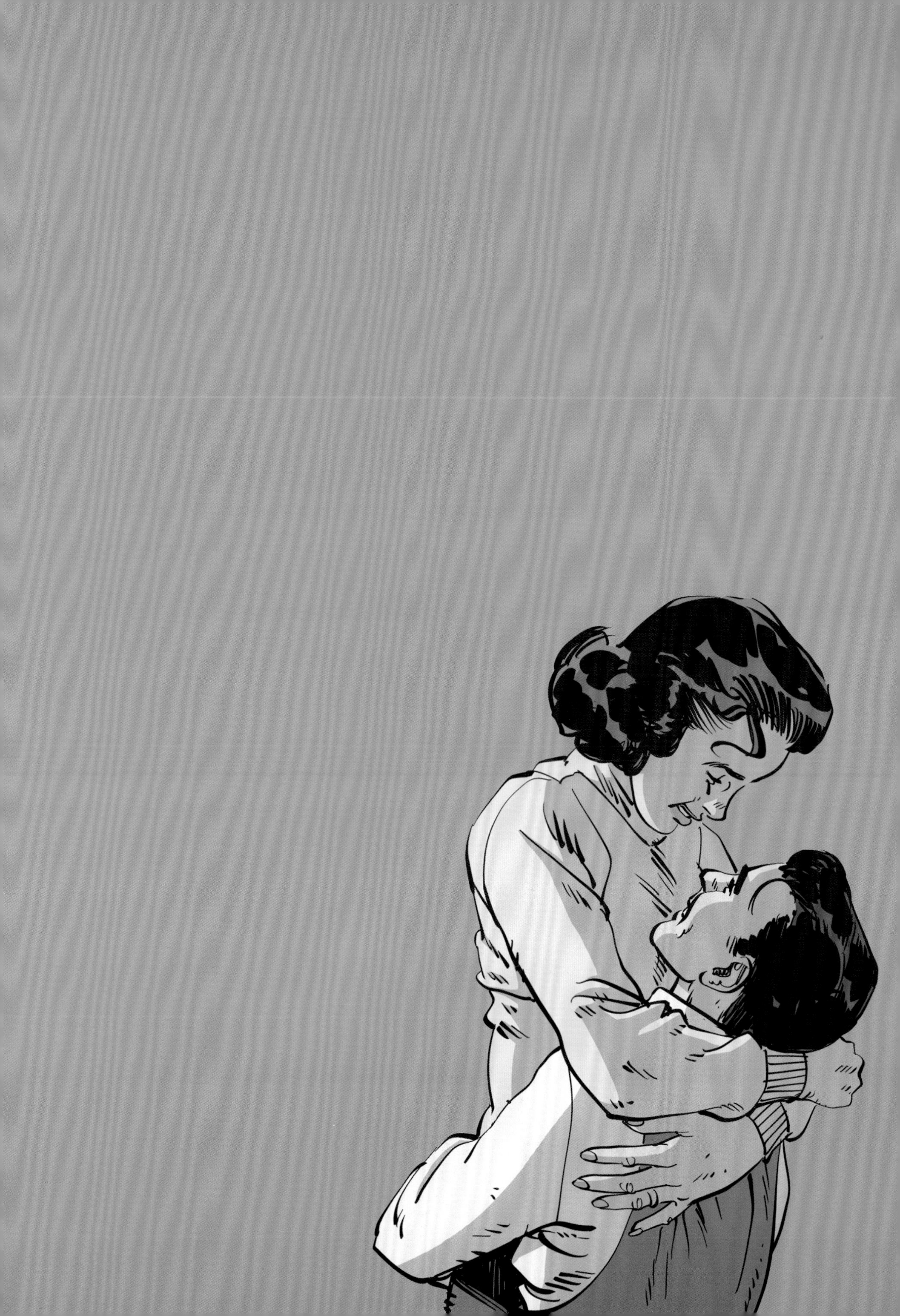

By the same authors

Balkans Arena

Other books by Philippe Thirault

Mandalay
With Butch Guice, Gallur & José Malaga

Miss: Better Living Through Crime
With Marc Riou & Mark Vigouroux

Robert Silverberg's Colonies: Return to Belzagor
With Laura Zuccheri

Sanctum Genesis
With Christophe Bec & Stefano Raffaele

The Hounds of Hell
With Christian Højgaard, Drazen Kovacevic & Roman Surzhenko

Thousand Faces
With Marc Males, Mario Janni & Paul Pope

Other books by Jorge Miguel

Orion's Outcasts
With Corbeyran & Julia Verlanger

The Z Word
With Jerry Frissen & Guy Davis